The Secret of Mem

The Secret of Mem

What Others Have Said about "The Secret of Mem"

"Your writing style and your 'Godly' insights gives us all food for thought; lovingly and positively prodding us all to wake up and become more cosmically aware."

Michael W. Hall, J.D.

"The Secret of Mem is a very well written book in which the narrative challenges the reader's understanding of the relationship between spiritual issues through God on one hand and science on the other through the role of time in the functioning of the universe. Readers are also challenged to understand the role of the "little black book" in guiding the process."

Delon Hanson

"And yet another of Richard Haines' extremely creative and entertaining novels. Coming from a man with a great reputation and career in social science, we are now graced with an engaging story that challenges the very core of belief. But not in a way that you'd expect. Instead you find yourself participating in a thought experiment of sorts that raises fundamental questions about reality and life as we know it by engaging us with a fresh mindset and unique backdrop of a hypothetical planet in your focus—and not the presumed comfortable backdrop of the Earth that you think you know! It's a provocative entertaining adventure!"

Michael Brein, Ph.D.

"A fascinating read – and scarily prescient for someone who actually suffers from transient amnesia of short duration that occurs in the "every few months" time frame. I found myself painfully able to identify with characters who were both waking up, and the 'care givers' assisting them in their recovery."

Charles D. Edwards, MSN|Ed, RN

The author, Richard Haines, a retired NASA scientist and serious student of the Word of God, has created in The Secret of Mem, a thoughtful allegory expounding the power of faith. The main character, William Thomas, finds the path to faith through the suppression of self-pride and self-doubt, and a renewed belief that God can be found in each of us, thereby achieving true freedom and consciousness. The Secret of Mem follows the path taken by William in his quest to solve another mystery surrounding Warren Wheaton, and his personal return to faith in a higher power, and what that can mean for all the inhabitants of the planet.

The ability to see our own modern society in this story makes it well worth the read, and gives one much to think about.

Kim Efishoff, Nuclear Engineer (U.S. Dept. of the Navy), Environmental Engineer (U.S. Dept. of Energy), Ret.

I enjoyed entering the world of Mem again while reading "The Secret of Mem." If you have never read Haines' first book, "The Pie of Mem," you should. The writing style of both will allow you to see everything in your mind's eye. And be prepared for a journey in "The Secret of Mem;" you will feel fear, struggle, and even ultimate encouragement throughout the book. I highly recommend "The Secret of Mem." It needs to be on your bookshelf.

Nathan P. Davis

Other Books by the Author

Justifications and Philosophy of the Space Age (1963)

UFO Phenomena and the Behavioral Scientist (1979)

Observing UFOs (1980)

Melbourne Episode: Case Study of a Missing Pilot (1987)

Advanced Aerial Devices Reported During the Korean War (1990)

Night Flying (with C. Flatau) (1992)

Project Delta: A Study of Multiple UFO (1994)

Close Encounters of the Fifth Kind – CE-5 (1999)

Sudden Loss: Earthquake Realities (2009)

Talking with Grandpa: A Personal Biography of Ancil Foster Haines (2018)

Paws and Christmas (with W. Stites) (2019)

The Bennetts of Plymouth, Michigan (2020)

The Pie of Mem (2020)

The Secret of Mem

A Land of Memories Sought

Richard F. Haines
Oak Harbor, Washington
June 2021

The Secret of Mem

ISBN - 9798746433770
Available from KindleDirect.Amazon
Charleston, SC
and local retail outlets
www.amazon.com/books
Printed in the United States of America
rev.

Front Cover Background: Philippe Donn 12578 (pexels.com)
Cover art work: Win Stites
Cover Layout: Karin Black

Preface

"Is this the world we have to accept?"

As we shall see, *The Secret of Mem* is mostly about memory and its frailties. Yet, there is another dimension of this story that is invisible and yet central to life - one's faith. As we will see, only with eyes of faith can one really perceive new truths, gain greater wisdom and experience truly life-changing events.

This story takes place on a small obscure recently discovered planet called *Mem* in the constellation Carina whose brightest star is Canopus. The mythological beginnings of this particular constellation (from earth's point of view at least) included Argo the ship of the Argonauts. And because Canopus is the second-brightest star both in our night sky as well as *Mem's* the inhabitants of that planet found it particularly useful in their early ocean navigations. *Memlandians* were as fascinated with the vast nighttime sights of their heavens as earthlings.

And, as we shall also see, its people are quite like humans except for their problems with memnesia, i.e., periodic losses of memory and time that require them to come up with many creative ways to cope with life's challenges.

The shape, geography, political divisions, and other features of the planet *Mem* have been described elsewhere (*The Pie of Mem*, 2020) so that only a brief review is presented here. This is where we shall begin.

Richard F. Haines
Oak Harbor, Washington

Prologue

A letter along with other typed pages
discovered in Warren's office desk at home

Dearest Wini,

If I should die before you here is something that I want you to read. I share these words of mine with you because they reflect the wisdom that came to me from a meeting I had with a very wise man during my participation on the Round-Mem-Expedition that you will remember.

I know that what I type next may not make much sense to you now but it will in time. Please keep these thoughts safe and share them only with those you trust.

I love you so much,

War

"We have lost so much time and for what? Although it is so fundamental, so foundational to everything that exists on Mem it still hides from us even now, like a delitescent jungle animal that is never caught, never tamed, never seen and cannot be controlled. For we Memlandians, this jungle animal may not be invisible at all; it is we who are blind. And why do we show so much indifference and arrogance toward our loss? Is it because we are unconsciously ignoring its Creator-who is our God?"

"Whatever time is it is far greater than any of us. It cannot be tamed in any way for we continue to lose it minute by minute even while we try to grasp it. Time is a primary attribute of Him who created it. Wini, thoughts about this wondrous hidden jungle animal have filled my mind for a long time."

"Could the shape of our prowling beast be that of a line, a two-dimensional creature with only a beginning and an end, a head and tail, a snake? Yet even a line drawn on paper need not be linear as time is. It can curve and cross-upon itself and even end where it begins. Can time be as unconstrained as this? The string theory of our ancients tried to force time into this wondrous complex mold without success."

"And is time's unidirectionality due only to God's wise kindness or to something else? Is He really showing His loving kindness for us on Mem by not permitting us to know what our future holds? Might God have some other hidden purpose in allowing time to flow out from Him in only one direction and not in reverse so that we might, ultimately, return to Him? Could this be yet another kindness, another reflection of God's nature? For whom among us wants to know the date or moment of his death? Yet mercifully, God has limited our life span in order to limit the evil that we might do-it is truly wise that all despots must die eventually. And why has He given us brains with a memory for past events but not for future ones? These questions are tiresome indeed."

"And the jungle creature I call time creeps on no matter how hard we try to guide his course, his speed, and the inevitable

consequences of his presence. We do this ignorantly, arrogantly, even piously until our own personal time runs out and the jungle animal finally leaves us."

"Indeed, time is so fundamental that it must be independent of all other known physical and mental elements."

"And what if time isn't just passing us by as we Memlandians commonly believe? What if it is continually being created and expanding into cosmic space to fill the whole Universe and thereby increase manifold entropy even more? What if it isn't simply another second of time that has been in existence all the time and then suddenly pops into view sixty times every minute? No! Rather, what if it's an entirely brand-new, freshly created second made to fill the void that was created by the disintegrating, ever-fleeing jungle animal?

And, what if time, space and energy do comprise dimensions of God Himself? It would not preclude Him from existing beyond them as well. Some call this His extradimensional Omnipresence and Omnipotence. And, where is God right now? Some call this place "heaven" which is clearly a spatial word. Others call it "eternity," a temporal word. If both of these are true then it's possible that without God there can be neither time nor space. Can there be a Creation without a Creator? Can there be existence without time? Without them I cannot even exist to write these words to you.

Dear Wini, there's something extremely mysterious about these matters."

Table of Contents

1

The Planet Mem

Mem is the name of a rather strange planet. As most planets go it was small and almost out of reach from Earth's ever-searching telescopes and orbiting satellites. It had only been detected by chance. One day an astronomer on earth had noticed its almost momentary silhouette as it passed directly in front of its own small sun. Later it was found that the probability of this same eclipse event happening by chance would take place only once in every one thousand eight-hundred and forty years and even then, there would have to have been someone looking in just the right direction at just the right time. It was this astronomically small chance occurrence that made it possible to write this book about *Mem*.

Mem's presence was later confirmed by a very small gravitationally related red shift of the spectrum of another nearby star. After considering both of these events carefully astronomers announced their preliminary discovery of a *probable* life-supporting planet only 1.3 light years away from Earth. This was much closer to earth than the far larger star Alpha Centauri which is about 4.37 light-years away and might possibly have its own satellites. Indeed, the distance to *Mem* was almost within reach of earth's unmanned space efforts.

Although this new planet was quite small relative to most other known planets its diameter was still almost twice as large as earth's. Astronomers were perplexed by another very odd characteristic. *Mem* wasn't spherical! Its surface was flat! Headlines of this discovery injected an exciting and fresh new spirit into members of the Flat Earth Society. So, with an estimated diameter of twenty-three thousand five hundred seventy-two miles, a circumference of just over seventy-four thousand fifty-three miles, and a thickness of just under six thousand two hundred miles, *Mem* would appear something like a very thick coin floating in space. Its reputation grew accordingly and produced a marked rush of excitement among earth's celestially focused crowd.

They also discovered that *Mem* orbited a sun of almost the same class as earth's yet it was slightly smaller in diameter; its wavelengths and radiant power were consistent with the kind of life-sustaining biochemistry humans know about. And because the distance to its sun and the number of days it took to orbit it was almost the same as that of earth's it strongly suggested a much higher possibility for sentient life being there. Later, when some astrophysicists had discovered a large proportion of liquid water on its surface, they were even more convinced. That single discovery turned out to be more exciting than all the others because water is absolutely essential for life forms as we know them. The discovery of water provided the pivot point for a great many telescopes and electro-magnetic-gravitational sensors to suddenly swing toward *Mem*! Using earth's most powerful telescope *Mem* appeared something like this.

Yes, *Mem* wasn't spherical at all. It had two opposing flat sides, something like a gigantic truck tire. It presented an irregularly shaped land mass surrounded by a huge ocean that moved slowly counterclockwise. Perhaps the planet was flat on its opposite side but earth's space and ground telescopes along with her many deep space satellites weren't able to tell for sure because it only presented one side toward earth.

It wasn't long before several astronomers announced that they had detected signs of life as well. Soon thereafter a particularly clear image of *Mem's* surface was obtained at great magnification. It showed very promising hints of sentient life! The news was electric and helped to greatly increase space research funding.

It was *Mem's* massive thickness that provided the downward pull of gravity over its entire surface. Its thickness and gravity were almost constant everywhere. *Mem's* gravitational force was something like time itself-invisible, constant, absolutely important. In one way or another almost everything the inhabitants on this strange planet did relied on this wondrous and completely taken-for-granted gravitational force. It kept water in their drinking glasses, caused rain to fall downward, helped stabilize vertical structures, made locomotion by animals and people possible, kept the ocean waters from falling off its edge and played a huge number of other vitally important roles.

To *Memlandians* (the people of *Mem*) time, a little like gravity, was a silently flowing invisible stream of another kind. A team of investigators on *Mem* had found that it passed at a constant rate everywhere on the planet. Earlier, curious scholars had proposed that the periodic loss of memory and time that every *Memlandian* experienced (as described below) was caused by deviations in the passage of time in various places around *Mem*. Field research had squelched their idea.

Memlandia was the planet's continental landmass. It was generally round with a vast ocean encircling it. It was actually a huge island continent fascinating for its natural diversity and beauty. And although the land was basically flat it still had hills and even some mountains with foothills, much like earth. Over countless eons erosion had scoured out its coastline; it boasted deep coves and protected harbors, smooth, white sandy beaches and atoll-like sharp rock outcroppings that posed dangers to shipping, tall precipitous landfalls into the sea, and many other inspiring features that are found where ever ocean and land meet.

Memlandia itself was almost eleven thousand miles across at its widest point with an area of about ninety-five million, one hundred sixty-two thousand, four hundred and sixty square miles. More importantly, its landmass was divided into three equal area (like slices of a pizza pie) for cultural, political and economic reasons.

Mem's ocean, called *Surging Waters,* was more than four times larger in area than the land which boasted many beautiful fresh-water rivers, streams and lakes, cascading water-falls, marshes and ponds as well as all kinds of wildlife and climates.

The three boundary lines dividing this *Pie of Mem* converged at the center of the pie. It was called the Compole (for 'common pole'). It had been dedicated long before as an international park "To BRING NATURE to FAMILIES and FAMILIES to NATURE" as a newspaper headline had announced many decades before.

Just as the geology, flora and fauna and everything else on *Mem* was similar to earth in many ways much the same could be said for its inhabitants. Eons of time had produced a hardy people who had survived severe weather, great floods and forest-fires, powerful earth-quakes, tsunamis, volcanic eruptions, magnificent hurricanes and droughts, dust bowls, insect plagues, pandemics and other kinds of natural disasters. Yes, the inhabitants of *Mem* survived, prospered and grew in population through them all.

For reasons now long since forgotten these peoples had gradually formed themselves into three nations. The first was called *Daytun* with a population of 11.12 million people. The second was *Weeklun* with 9.96 million souls and the third was *Yurland* with 10.71 million.

. . .

Most *Daytunians* considered themselves a hardy, outdoor-loving people. They loved their freedom from: heavy-handed politics (being the most politically independent and libertarian in spirit of the three countries), high taxes and bland foods (most of them actually loved spicy specialty foods the best). In general, they were also the most sensual in that they loved their many creature comforts that technology, electricity, and commerce had provided them. Finally, they also loved competition sports of all kinds.

Anthropologists and psychologists who studied *Daytunian* culture discovered that they ranked lowest of all *Memlandians* in several areas such as: long-term goal achievement, social skills, general intelligence and motivational drive. None of the experts could discover what could have caused these characteristics because all of the likely reasons for one country to differ from another (such as nutrition, genetic makeup, health condition and other life-span determining factors), were basically the same.

Nevertheless, the most important distinguishing characteristic of every *Daytunian*-man, woman and child-was that he or she lost all sense of time and memory around noon every day of every week of every year. Virtually all cognitive conscious functions simply stopped for a while. Everyone entered their daily memnesia period, as it was called, sometime near noon. The entire country came to a virtual halt. The most fortunate citizens were unconscious for only about five minutes a day while others were “out” for up to two hours! The average was thirty-eight minutes. It’s not hard to understand why those born with the shortest durations of cognitive oblivion were hired before others and rose a little higher up the socio-economic scale.

People on *Mem* called their dysfunction by many names: “memnesia,” “period of blankness,” “memory dysfunction” (MD for short), “prisoner of noon,” ”oblivion,” “my missing time,” and others that can’t be printed here. A few *Daytunians* wanted to have it classified as a clinical fugue state so that they could qualify for free national medical support, slightly lower health insurance rates or both. Others were so bold as to claim they entered into dementia with their real or imagined symptoms of agitation, restlessness, anxiety, and even hallucinations. But officials quickly recognized these attempts for the scams they were and didn't allow them. This daily cognitive dysfunction led to many challenges for the *Daytunians* as they went about their daily lives.

Everyone was prohibited from driving any kind of motor vehicle as noontime approached. Bus and taxi drivers had to stop and pull over at least five minutes before their own period of blankness began. Sometimes this caused accidents, traffic jams and disrupted transportation schedules. While automobile drivers were supposed to do the same for the good of themselves and everyone else, some didn't. This led to serious collisions yet not as many pedestrian accidents since almost everyone in the country was immobile and insensible at the time. Visitors from the other nations who happened to be walking the streets of *Daytun* around noon quickly learned to stay alert for what were basically driverless cars and trucks.

Of course, the same rules applied to piloting airplanes. *Daytun's* official Department of Transportation prohibited all flights during the daytime hours of eleven fifteen a.m. and three p.m. To be licensed, commercial pilots were carefully screened to make sure that only those having the shortest durations of daily amnesia were accepted. Pilots were only allowed to fly with paying passengers if their airplanes had automated flight control systems on board (called auto-pilots) that could fly the airplane all by itself if the pilot became unconscious in flight. These amazing flight instruments were carefully programmed to take control of the airplane at least ten minutes before the known start time of the flight crew's loss of consciousness. (The long and drawn-out legal wrangling and controversies that surrounded the approval of commercial airline operations beyond *Daytun's* borders aren't described here). Of course, airline management tried to hire cockpit crews whose duration and onset of memnesia was not only short but very consistent and well documented. Private piloting was another matter.

Private pilots were permitted to fly any time of the day or night but had to prove they had a large amount of insurance coverage since so many had crashed around noon. Since driving cars and flying a private airplane was a personal choice many did so even though they knew they risked injury and death.

Many amateur and professional sports leagues were established in *Daytun* because everyone loved sports of every kind. While international matches were held every year, they were not permitted to be played around noon. If they had been the crowds in the stands would have grown ominously quiet at noon which would have dispirited the teams on the field, some of whom might also have been immobile and senseless.

And when it came to dealing with criminal activity *Daytun's* police departments discovered that criminals possessing shorter memnesia periods were robbing and assaulting other people who were still unconscious and unable to protect themselves. The list of such social problems faced by *Daytunians* was as long as it was complex.

Indeed, their memnesia caused many other problems for its citizens as might be imagined; they finally convinced their government officials to seek various remedies. One of these was the memory dysfunction bracelet-affectionately called the 'MD band'. It had been invented as a personal safety measure to inform emergency responders who happened upon people who appeared unconscious or asleep. Everyone born in *Daytun* over the age of sixteen had to wear one on their wrist. It was distributed free by the government. Deeply embossed on its shiny metallic surface was the day of the week and approximate duration of everyone's memnesia. Made of polished plated gold or silver, the thin plain band was not unattractive yet some still wore it with embarrassment, particularly when they visited friends in *Weeklun* or *Yurland.* Others viewed the bracelet as a kind of one-armed handcuff that wouldn't allow them to forget that they forgot. Many viewed themselves as prisoners of their own government as much as of their own minds.

Nevertheless, like citizens of the other two countries on *Mem, Daytunians* had developed ways to cope as best they could with their own daily periods of missing time and memory. Truly, the clock ruled their nation as well as it did the entire planet.

But what about the nation of *Weeklund* to the west? Every *Weeklunder* experienced the same memnesia symptoms as did their neighbors not daily but weekly; actually, once every seven days around noon. For some it occurred on Monday, others on Tuesday, and so on. Sociologists teamed up with anthropologists and discovered that the particular day on which it occurred didn't correspond with the day of that person's birth. That finding didn't do the credibility of astrologers very much good. Studies found that the shortest period of memory loss was about ten minutes while the longest was twenty-four hours. The national average was around fifty minutes!

They were a clever people who tried many different things to cope with their dilemma. For some denial served them well. It was easy for them to simply view their missing time as if it had never happened and focus only on what occurred after they had returned to so-called "normal" consciousness. Yet, ignoring something that was unconscious wasn't even possible without there being solidly-remembered bookends that marked the start and end of each MD period. If they were injured in some way while they were "out" they had no recollection of how it happened nor did they feel pain afterward. It was as if the source of the memnesia also produced a prolonged and welcome anesthetic effect.

Those who were good at making up alibis for their missing time and memory loss constructed elaborate stories that diverted the attention of others or at least distracted them with absurd, made-up facts. This mechanism wasn't very popular, though, because it led to losing those friends who could see through their false stories.

For some *Weeklunders*, putting on an act of innocence about their missing time seemed to work. Much like denial, this response relied on experiences that occurred just before or after the MD period to fill in the missing gap. Some people made fun of those who used this approach even though they might do the same thing. Their friends and acquaintances were left wondering how the person could be so naïve, so infantile, as to pretend innocence in this way?

Jealousy served still others as a useful overt cover. If someone else was known to lose their memory for a shorter length of time than oneself it was easy to become jealous of them and the "advantage" that they had been born with. Of course, feelings of jealousy can work in both directions and some *Weeklunders* resented the snide terse comments that they received.

A few *Weeklundians* used humor to cope. They found ways to laugh at themselves and others particularly when they forgot to attend meetings, left home on an errand then returned home empty-handed, and otherwise acted like brainless people.

The last group simply got angry at others when they arrived late for a meeting or forgot a name. Their misdirected anger not only indicted themselves, it got them into difficulties as we shall see.

In virtually all other ways one couldn't tell a *Weeklunder* from anyone else on the planet.

Memnesia was hard to cope with on the best of days so when stress or personal troubles built up in one's life their abrupt and total loss of consciousness only added to their challenges and contributed to their misery. While at night they could go to sleep at any time they chose and feel rested when they woke up their interruption in the middle of their work day became a source of great difficulty.

• • •

Yurland was the third country of *Mem.* Other than some differences with its two neighbors in terms of its greater national productivity and wealth, higher standard of living and education it was indistinguishable from them. Only when one examined their challenge of memnesia did this difference become obvious.

A *Yurlander's* memory debility had a positive and a negative side. On the positive side they led normal lives for a full three hundred sixty-four days before their cognitive lapse began; the day, week and month on which it happened varied from person to person. This long span of uninterrupted time and useful memory, except for sleep of course, allowed them to take full advantage of their uninterrupted time. Many citizens became highly-skilled engineers, architects, scientists, medical personnel, and other professional occupations; over time significantly more of these high-income occupations developed there than in *Weeklun* or *Daytun.* This contributed to the nation's higher standard of living.

On the negative side was the long duration of their oblivion. Although it happened only once a year it lasted about two and one-half months on average!

The longest recorded period of someone's memory debility was one year, five months, six days, and eleven hours! That poor person couldn't account for over half of his life.

Because of their very long periods of memnesia (being virtually unconscious) many who were without family members or spouses required special in-home care givers whose own period of oblivion had to be different from theirs. Professional care giving became a thriving business.

Another business that did exceedingly well was psychiatry because of the mental strains that were suffered by missing life over such long periods of time. Some *Yurlanders* who had to provide continuous technical advice or support services to others all year-such as financial advisors and public servants-found themselves increasingly frustrated, anxious, fearful, and even angry when they had to give up their jobs for a prolonged span after a year-long span of working.

Another more hidden problem that *Yurlanders* faced was that when one went unconscious for so long a period of time, they couldn't defend themselves from robbery or physical assault by those who weren't unconscious or had been blessed with shorter periods of memory dysfunction (MD). Because of this *Yurland* had the highest crime rate on *Mem*.

Because *Yurland's* policemen also suffered from periods of MD officer selection favored either "short timers" as they were called (men and women who were incapacitated for no more than a couple of weeks each year) or, more frequently, foreigners with much shorter but more frequent periods of memnesia. Police units were formed and scheduled carefully. Indeed, *Daytunian* criminals did their best to take advantage of this weakness of the police.

Needless to say, the citizens of *Yurland* faced other challenges as well. A well-known nutritionist discovered that its citizens consumed considerably less magnesium than did the peoples of *Daytun* or *Weeklun*. Geologists uncovered the reason why. Their soil contained over twenty percent less of this element than elsewhere on *Mem*. They reasoned that this deficiency might be related to their very long yearly bouts of memnesia.

Realizing that these challenging episodes of cognitive lapse had taken place gradually over many centuries it's understandable that *Memlandians* considered them to be a normal part of life, much as they viewed their sleep. While the early inhabitants on *Mem* had looked for cures more recent folks simply accepted their memnesia as a normal part of life. These periods of missing time and memory were so deeply entrenched and familiar that by instinct the people did nothing to eliminate them. Their brains simply refused to acknowledge them. Some called it the result of their normalcy bias.

2

Old Memories are Best

Winifred Wheaton sat on the edge of her bed looking at nothing except the thin shafts of sunlight that had slipped into her room between the narrow parallel blinds and then been absorbed into the oval braid of her carpet. She was unaware of their slow but steady progression toward her feet because her mind was numbed, still paralyzed by overwhelming grief of her loss that blotted out everything else. The sun, also quite unaware, crossed the sky slowly toward the western horizon but she didn't care. Its yellow-orange strands of light had no meaning, no significance at all. Her spirit was close to death; it hadn't the strength even to allow the pain of her loss to reach her heart much less her mind. There was no way sunlight could illuminate her soul because Warren had left her so suddenly, so unexpectedly.

"How could he have done that to me?" she cried out in anger. "He died only last week in that terrible automobile accident that had killed the other driver as well."

Wini had always considered herself to be a strong and self-reliant woman. Now almost sixty years old with strands of greying hair, she still possessed an attitude of, "Yes, I can, I'm able to..." along with an impressive list of journalistic skills honed by almost three decades of on-the-job experience. Together, these traits had kept her diligently employed at the local newspaper for many years. That had helped them stay ahead of the bills. And, packed away in a faint corner of her mind, she knew that she had tried to be a good wife to Warren but now she wasn't as sure.

The room's somber darkness was welcome for it submerged her hidden emotions even deeper on this Thursday mid-morning. She couldn't bring herself to open the curtains even when she began to hear the sounds of rain drops tapping lightly on her window pane. "Thank you, God for crying with me." She could not bear to face another day of heavy associations.

It was her day of the week to lose her memory for about forty minutes; the discrete official government MD bracelet she wore on her left wrist forever linked its day and duration to her in case emergency personnel should find her lying in a coma or unconscious from an apparent stroke. But today she was actually looking forward to her fore-ordained release from the frightful memory of his death and desertion. Her forty minutes of oblivion would be a blessing.

As she was about to descend into her period of insensibility, she thought about whether she really had been a good a wife over their many years of marriage. Her mind seemed to flit from one memory to another in no particular order.

"I've got to concentrate," she said to herself. "I remember our first meeting. He was only thirty-one and really a nice guy although he did have a temper. He wasn't flashy or forward, that was one of the things I liked so much about him." But as her mind tried to focus on the Warren she knew and loved it shifted once again; the time just wasn't right... yet.

As she sat there her phone began to ring; it startled her out of her reverie and back into the reality of her grief. She reached for the bedside stand and picked it up.

"Hello? Oh, hi Danielle, it's really nice of you to call."

"Hi from Duncan and me. We've been thinking about you since we read about, about the accident. Are you OK?" she asked.

"Yes I'm doing fairly well under the circumstances," she lied. "I really don't need anything." Wini understood that people felt compelled to call and share their own mixture of feelings, thinking that the bereaved would surely feel better because of their call. Wini understood this and tried hard to make an allowance for Danielle's insensitivity. "Well, I've been better and I think I'll get through this but, you know, I miss him so much." She began to cry.

Danielle was sorry she had called.

Danielle asked, "Could I bring anything over? A meal, a bottle of wine? Would it help to get out of the house? She thought that all the memories the house contained probably would be hard on Wini.

"No, I don't think I'll get out of the house for a while, why did you ask?"

"It's just that if I were you I'd like to have some companionship, that's all."

"Oh, that would be wonderful but give me another week or so, OK? Things will get better but it will take time." Wini said bravely. "It's nice hearing from you. Give my love to Duncan will you. Tell him I look forward to calling him professor. OK? So long Danielle."

"Goodbye. Oh, and I almost forgot, I wanted to thank you and Warren so much for what you shared with Duncan and me at our reunion." (The two couples had met at Compole Inn several months before for a reunion during which Wini and Warren had shared how important it is to know God personally and to invite Him into one's heart and home and, more importantly, about how to actually go about doing it). "We both talked about your advice a lot and we've been doing it. Our lives together are already much better. Thank you both so much. And so, I'll just say so long for now." They hung up.

Wini was glad at what she heard. Both Warren and she had spoken truth to them independently, without any prior agreement or planning between them; strangely enough, both had shared almost the same words. The special message Wini had shared came from her own marriage. Danielle's news boosted her spirit a little, for a few minutes at least.

The bedside clock read eleven-fifty a.m. She felt relieved that her MD hadn't happened during her phone call. Fortunately, or unfortunately, even at sixty, she still had a sharp memory; she remembered the early stages of what was about to happen to her and decided to just give in and let it happen again as she lay on her bed. She knew there was nothing she could do about it anyway.

But at other times when she had the energy, she would try to fight her submersion into the familiar void of nothingness. She didn't want to be mastered by this uncontrollable enemy and fought it any way she could. But in the end, it always had its way. Sometimes when she was at work at noon she stayed at her desk as if her intense mental concentration might somehow overcome her plunge into the deep pool of timelessness. At other times, like when she went out driving near noontime on Thursdays, she would only pull over and stop at the last possible moment when she felt the early signs coming on. Several times it had almost cost her her life. But it didn't matter. She was fiercely determined to be a survivor not a victim.

As noon finally arrived she was ready, stretched out and relaxed on their queen sized bed thinking about all those past times when she and Warren had lain there together deep in serious conversations about life, how best to raise their two daughters and what the future held for them, his job at the police department, and hers at the paper.

Just as she was recalling a conversation about how he had been secretly planning something exciting and fun for their next vacation she recognized the telltale, low toned pitch in her ears that always signaled the onset of her "time out," as she called it. After a few more seconds she felt slightly dizzy and closed her eyes. She had learned the hard way that keeping them open could leave her feeling very disoriented and nauseated. Then another sensation began, something like tingling from a weak electrical shock. It started at her feet and crept slowly upward to her chest where she became aware of her rapidly increasing heart rate. Then, without any noticeable pause at her chest level, the tingling rose into her head. Then she was out.

Wini's weekly "time out" left no embedded traces of any kind. For her it was like sleep without dreams or sensations of any kind. She had compared the symptoms she could remember with several other women at work and was relieved to learn that God, or whomever had planned it, had spared her many of the unpleasant sensation's others said they experienced. Some of her friends described troubling attacks of anxiety during their periods of missing time and memory dysfunction. For other *Weeklunders* their symptoms were those of a senseless robot who could walk and even talk but process nothing mentally, recall nothing. To another person they would appear like a human puppet who didn't speak the language, know the customs or react appropriately.

It was forty minutes past noon when she eventually climbed back up out of her memory dysfunction period as she usually did.

"Oh yes, I'm at home and I'm safe yet I don't remember anything about what I was doing before," she thought. "I'd better get up or the rest of the day will slip by as well."

She got up unsteadily and walked to the phone in the kitchen. Ever since that awful night when she heard the news of his traffic accident, she had hated that beige-colored object on the counter. It seemed to bring her more bad news than good. But she remembered something she needed to do. She dialed the Chief of Police of Morristown where Warren had been a detective. The phone rang only twice before it picked up.

"Hello, this is Mrs. Wheaton, Warren's wife and I'd like to speak with the chief." All right, "I'll wait."

Only seconds later she heard his voice, "Hello Winifred. I'm so glad to hear from you. I hope you're all right."

"Yes, but I'm still not fully back to normal. It's been a rough several weeks," she replied.

"I can understand," he said, his voice becoming lower and softer.

Wini thought to herself, "How could he understand? He's never lost someone he loved." Out loud she said, "uh, well... the reason I'm calling is... to see if we could meet sometime?" She heard nothing for several long seconds. She thought he was probably wondering why she wanted to meet.

The chief finally said, "Sure. I'd be glad to only it will have to wait several days if that's OK, my schedule is really full right now."

"Oh, that would be fine. How about next Monday then, in the mid-afternoon?"

The chief paused as he checked his calendar and then replied, "Yes, that works for me. And where would you like to meet?"

Wini answered, "Well, there's a small restaurant about two blocks from your office on Shay Street. Do you know it?"

"Yes, how about two o-clock?"

"Thank you, I'll be there." Both hung up.

. . .

The lunch crowd at this late hour had left only four other customers finishing their drinks and food when Wini arrived at one fifty-five p.m. She was relieved to find that the place stayed open through to the dinner hour, not that she needed that much time to tell the chief what she had to say.

It was touted as an ethnic restaurant with a menu that gathered recipes together from earlier times, times when there weren't preservatives or refrigeration, genetically modified molecules, electric ovens or many dietary fads. It also specialized in *Yurland's* and *Daytun's* cuisine not that there was that much difference. She had never been to the place before but had heard about it from her boss at work. She was glad he recommended it. Its deep rich aromas were comforting somehow.

Its cozy closed atmosphere gave her a sense of calm and greater security. She didn't know why that seemed so important today for this meeting in particular but it was. There were only ten tables present each seating four with starched white tablecloths, a tall vase of colorful hot-house flowers in the middle, a set of two candles in cut-glass orbs to flicker in each customers' liquid refreshments, and silver place settings and napkins, really quite elegant and even romantic, something she needed.

She had chosen a table near the stone fireplace with its glowing wood coals and low, flickering, crackling flame. A small stack of split logs on the hearth gave it an authenticity that other restaurants didn't have. It added real warmth to the welcome charm of the room. Only two other tables were occupied at this late lunch hour.

Several minutes later the chief walked in through the front door in his uniform and spied her in the back. A waiter smiled and nodded as he walked by. "He's a good customer... tips well," he thought to himself.

"Hello Wini... right on time," he began as he glanced around the rest of the restaurant looking for any familiar faces. There were none. He sat down opposite her and went on, "I've always been a prompt man. I value being punctual. It's a mark of respect for the other person more than anything else you know."

She smiled and nodded. She was glad for his forthright and friendly beginning, nothing negative or heavy about him. She had interviewed a great many people over her years as a newspaper reporter and knew how to gauge someone's emotions pretty fast.

"And I'm so glad that you're doing so well after... since Warren passed away... I know it was a terrible blow," he went on looking down and shaking his head slowly. He knew that she was still grieving but she was also a reporter. Did she have some inside news for him? He managed to not let his curiosity become too obvious.

"It was the hardest thing I'll ever go through," she responded, "I mean his sudden death in that terrible accident. That's partly why I wanted to talk with you."

He searched her eyes for some warmth, some inner flame but he found almost none. He could tell that she was still in shock. He smiled and leaned forward as he said, "Wini. You know how much I respected Warren. He was a fine detective; he'd served on the force for many years and never stopped looking for new ways to learn and advance himself. More than that, I can tell you that we became friends as well. We spent a lot of time talking about life and many other things."

She smiled weakly and gazed down at the perfectly smoothly ironed tablecloth just as a waiter approached to take their order. They both ordered coffee.

The chief went on, "You know Wini, when you get to

my position you don't really have many true friends." He seemed a little embarrassed as he said this."

"Yes, I think I understand. I saw that happening between William and Warren over the years as well. Warren kind of took him on as a younger brother and encouraged him to become a detective too."

The chief's eyes squinted as his smile broadened. Tiny wrinkle lines spread out from the corners of his eyes. He said, "I know, I watched it from the inside. The two of them became thick as thieves." The chief knew that his job wasn't to carry out investigations himself but to marshal the forces and keep them focused in the right direction while finding ways to encourage and support them along the way. He chuckled briefly before going on. "Your husband turned out to be an exemplary detective you know. Both of those guys could think outside the box in difficult situations, but I'm rambling on. You called this meeting. So, what is it that I can do for you?"

Wini straightened up in her seat as their coffees arrived. After the waiter left, she said, "Well, it's about something that Warren said to me soon before he died."

He held his hand up and interrupted her, thinking he could make her task easier. He said, "I think I know what you're talking about. If you will, let me try to guess. Tell me if I'm right or wrong." He broke in thinking that it would help her, soften what she had to share.

"Several days before his accident the mayor and I both received several telephone calls from high level government officials in all three nations of *Mem*," he began, "All of them told us pretty much the same thing and I'm sure the callers hadn't talked with one another beforehand. They said that Warren had called them a day or two before his accident. Each said that he sounded very excited and, after he introduced himself, he had that he had discovered a sure cure for our planet's periods of noontime amnesia and that he wanted to meet with them to share the details in the near future." He waited to see her response (The chief didn't mention that these officials thought they were dealing with a deranged person; they had received equally weird correspondences before this).

Her eyebrows raised. Her look of surprise was followed by a smile and then a brief nod. Although she didn't know anything about what the chief had just told her she went along with it as if she did. It was a technique she had learned over the years as a reporter to draw people out in order to share even more facts. His disclosure suddenly caused many things to fall into place in her mind.

She had no reason not to tell the chief everything she knew. He was a friend, trustworthy and clearly a highly respected *Weeklundian* official. He also had been fair and supportive of her husband. "So," she began, "That makes a lot more sense now. It fits in with how he had been acting at home for years, actually ever since he came back from a scientific expedition hiking around the planet years ago." Her mind was swirling uncontrollably as she remembered more and more things that had puzzled her about his behavior.

The chief interrupted, "Yes, I know about that. I approved his participation for that assignment."

"Assignment? What do you mean? I thought it was an independent project sponsored by *Memlandia* officials and scientists not the *Weeklun* Police Department."

"Let me explain," he began as he looked around the restaurant for anyone who might have been listening too closely. He lowered his voice even more and went on, "Well I thought that as long as he was going to be hiking through much of our countryside as well as the other two countries, I would assign him covertly to assist with a special criminal project we had underway.

I can only tell you this much... it had to do with the huge rise in smuggling we'd been experiencing and...", he stopped abruptly. He remembered that she was a newspaper reporter and he might have tipped her off to a juicy story. He said, "Wini, all this is off the record you understand. Our project is still active and we wouldn't want these criminal elements to learn anything they shouldn't. I'm sure you understand."

"Yes, of course, whatever you tell me today stays with me."

He went on, "Thanks, I appreciate that. As I was saying, Warren went on his expedition as an undercover investigator even though at the time he was only our chief files clerk as you know, long before he became a detective. Well, when he came back from that trip, we all noticed that something had happened to him. He was a brand-new man. You probably noticed the same thing."

She didn't reply but her thoughts flashed back to those days. They brought tears of happiness that clouded her vision. She recalled with a smile how Warren had suggested that, as co-equal marriage partners, each of them should make the major house-hold decisions together. Proverbially speaking, each should put one of their legs in the same pair of decision-making pants," he had said, "... and then walk forward together." She found herself laughing as she remembered how badly that idea had worked out on several occasions. Her tears and laughter were good for her, cathartic, cleansing.

The chief could tell that she was agreeing with him. He continued. "When I sat him down in my office to find out what had happened on the trip, he only laughed and grinned and acted like a school boy whose been sipping hard liquor. I think I felt more embarrassed at the time than he did. But he seemed so genuinely filled with a new joy for life that I'd never seen before that I just accepted it as some kind of temporary personality quirk; I thought it would probably dissipate over time and I certainly thought that you would also notice it. But it never did dissipate. Here at work he gradually calmed down a little and so I just dropped it."

"Yes. That's it exactly, a new joy. That's also what I saw in him but he never told me what had changed him. I even got in touch with the two men who went with him on that expedition but they didn't know the cause either. It was really strange... chief, that's really what I wanted to talk with you about."

He became serious for a moment as he leaned back in his chair and took a drink from his cup. Inside, he was getting more excited as well as curious by what he heard. "Perhaps she would disclose something more important, a piece of the larger puzzle that he and many of the detectives in the department had been wondering about. Perhaps it had something to do with the crime syndicate?

She went on, "Warren told me that he had met an old man. I think it was in central *Weeklun* and he had told him something important."

The chief broke in again, "I can tell you that he wrote about that meeting in his official trip report but it was a pretty short account as I remember."

She went on, "To me it sounded kind of religious or philosophical or something. Whatever it was I think it was related to his change of personality and I'm also more and more certain that something the old man said or did was the cause. Then some years later, as we were driving back home from a reunion with friends at Compole Park, he took me on a side-trip. It was along some back roads in search of something. Actually, it turned out to be someone. We turned in on an overgrown dirt road that led to a broken-down cabin; it seemed to me that he had been there before, it was familiar to him. I got out to walk near a nearby stream but he walked around and disappeared behind the cabin. When he finally came back, he had been crying. When I asked him about it, he broke down and explained that he had found the grave of the old man he had meet years before during their expedition. He was really broken up."

The chief was listening intently and taking mental notes. He thought to himself, "That's new information and jibes with some other details Warren had written down in his trip report. I need to reread it." He remained quiet; he didn't want to distract her.

Wini's eyes filled with tears yet again as she looked down at the tablecloth. She was struggling with long-cherished memories. After several more minutes of silence she finally went on, "Well, as I said, he was a brand-new man and I appreciated it so much. He was more attentive toward me, more accepting of my foibles you might say." She blushed as she admitted this. "Actually, I was glad that he had gone away and come back changed and I told him so. I also told him that I wished I could have gone away with him. I remember clearly that he didn't reply to that."

"Can I ask you a question Wini?"

"Yes, of course."

"Can you remember anything about what that old man told him or anything he did, anything at all?"

"No, not really, but it seemed like he was holding a secret inside himself, something that was terribly important," she answered. "At the same time, it was like he was carrying a great burden of joy and knowledge. That was what was so strange. He seemed joyous and yet burdened at the same time."

The chief only nodded.

"You see, to me Warren seemed to be in possession of something very valuable, no, powerful, that would be a better word for it, I think."

"Why did you use that word?" he asked.

"Well, it's because he wouldn't even tell me, his wife. At first, I was hurt and offended by his unwillingness to open up. But then I realized that his secret must be so big that he probably couldn't trust it to anyone. Eventually, I came to think that it was his way of protecting me."

"I see. Now let me get this straight, he never mentioned any kind of clues to you about his secret, as you called it?" he asked.

"That's right, as far as I can remember, it's been a long time ago you know. It's probably not very important but I sensed that the day before he died, he was really excited about something. I remember him telling me that he was going to tell me something at dinner. Maybe it was that secret... he never got the chance."

(Neither she or the chief knew that Warren had brought back a small black leather-bound book from his meeting with the old man he met in the forest. In it was a precious record of ancient wisdom about the cause, cure, and aftermath of the amnesia malady that had plagued *Mem* from the beginning of time. Neither of them could have guessed that Warren had read that volume over and over again, memorizing much of it, and had succeeded in applying its teachings to himself. He had been changed for the rest of his life. He was the only *Memlandian* who didn't suffer from memnesia.)

The chief thought for a while before speaking. He was deep in thought about several meetings he had had with Warren soon after he returned from that trip. Then he remembered that Warren had written up a detailed trip report. "I have to find it," he said to himself.

Wini said, "I guess that was really what I wanted to tell you. The whole thing has been a mystery to me and I hoped that you could explain what he was holding so dear. I thought that you would know."

"Wini I'm afraid I don't know anything more than you do but I'm determined to find out if I can."

Wini looked both relieved and concerned at the same time. She hadn't learned anything new but she felt the chief was now on her side, a seeker along with herself, an accomplice. Then she said, "I've got to get to the bottom of this. You don't think it's a bad idea to talk with William, his partner, do you?" She asked even though she had made up her mind to do it anyway.

The chief shook his head and replied, "No, not at all. In fact, I'm going to do the same thing in the near future." (What he didn't tell Wini was that his primary reason for getting involved in this search into Warren's past wasn't as much about his personality change as it was because he thought there might be some link with the criminal syndicate and their growing list of activities. Warren might have uncovered something else of value).

"I do thank you for your time today. It's been helpful for me and I hope something I've told you was as well," she said as she started to stand up to leave.

"Yes, I think it has and I appreciate your courage and strength as you're dealing with your loss... I should have said our loss. I will miss him too you know; but now I must get back to work," he said as he pushed back from the table and reached over for their bill and stood up.

"Goodbye Wini... until we meet again... and please call me if there's anything I can do for you."

"That's very kind of you, I will. Good bye."

. . .

Two more days passed before she had the courage to phone William. She found his name and phone number in Warren's phone file on his desk. For her, each day was a burden filled more with memories from the past than plans for the future. There were moments when she felt she had no future. At other times all she felt was a heaviness that pulled her down against her will, like an invisible pull of gravity. There was no trace of buoyant happiness. She was going through what all widows go through if they had truly loved their mate. But, she finally found the strength to dial his number and was surprised when he answered on the second ring.

"Hello?"

"William, this is Win... can we talk sometime soon?"

He was taken aback at her abrupt question and immediately went into detective mode. He thought, "What's happened? Why would she be calling me now? Is everything all right?" His thoughts turned into words. "Is everything OK Wini?"

In his younger years William had been a computer geek who literally dragged his avocation, his only all-consuming hobby, along behind him to college like a pet on a leash. He eventually earned a degree in computer science (he knew more than most of his professors). Soon after graduation he was hired by Morristown's Police Department as a Level 1 computer systems trainee. But, because of his obvious knowledge of current-day computer systems, software and specialized apps that dwarfed what the existing staff knew about he was promoted rapidly to Chief of Division 6, Computation. He met Warren several years later and struck up a friendship when Warren was still in charge of police files and the official evidence locker. The rest is history. The two applied to become detectives at the same time; Warren passed his exams but William didn't until sometime later. When he finally did, he was assigned as Warren's partner.

Hearing the voice of her husband's partner caused her to freeze for several seconds. Memories flooded back into her mind again: late night meetings around cups of hot black coffee or beers, the BBQs they had shared together, talking about their future hopes and dreams.

Warren and he had a close friendship built on mutual respect and trust. At length she said, “William, I didn’t mean to worry you or anything. It’s just that there are some questions I’d like to ask you. Would that be OK?”

“You know it would,” he replied, “anytime, anyplace, just say when and where.”

“Oh, thank you so much. I’ll tell you what they are about when we meet.”

. . .

Wini was walking toward the same small restaurant where she had met the chief the week before. It seemed like a good place to meet William. The chill in the air was heightened by the breeze that had begun to pick up. She was getting cold and decided to wait for him inside. Just as she reached the front door, she saw him running toward her across the street from where he had parked his unmarked police car. She wondered if a detective could get a ticket for jaywalking? He had found a parking place in spite of the fact that he didn’t really have to since he was still on official duty. He waved and called out with a grin, “Hi, how’s that for timing?” His smile made her feel warmer inside and safer, too.

“Hello William. It’s so good to see you again. Let’s go inside where we can talk… it’s cold out here.”

Once ensconced at a table at the rear of the small restaurant near its fireplace’s welcome warmth and gentle fire, she said, “I hope you’re not on duty now.”

“Well, yes I am but you’ll always take precedence over anything I need to be doing.”

“That’s so kind of you.” She knew he was being compassionate and didn’t really mean it literally; she had been married to Warren and knew the real limits of a detective’s personal time.

He wasted no time. “Wini, when you called it really

sounded urgent. Is there something I can do for you?" he said with a serious look on his face.

She smiled weakly. "That's exactly what your chief said to me last week." She studied his features and saw a young man in his thirties who looked much younger and, in a way, even naïve. He wasn't tall, but was well built, on the edge of being handsome. "Why hadn't he ever been snatched up by some woman?" she wondered. Out loud she said, "Not really. At least not right away. You see that since Warren died, I've been puzzled about something and I hope you could help me figure it out."

"OK, I will if I can." He had become more serious. His voice had lowered in pitch and in volume as if she was going to share some great secret.

"Let's order coffee first," she said. She needed time to organize her thoughts and present them in just the right way to William.

"All right. I'll see if I can catch the eye of our server over there." He had to wave several times before he finally succeeded; the waiter took their order for two black coffees and retreated again out of sight. "Now, please go on."

"Well, I'd better begin at the beginning," she began.

For the next fifteen minutes she told William the same information she had shared with the chief: how Warren had come back from his expedition a totally different and far more positive man, how he also seemed to be carrying a secret or something really heavy around within himself, a secret he wouldn't share with her... and also about the little old man he said he had met. She concluded, "William, can you help me? Did he ever tell you anything about what happened to him... about what had made such a big change in his life? I really need to know. It would be such a comfort and blessing to me."

William listened intently. He met Warren sometime

after his expedition and had read only one newspaper article about him and the trip. That article was partly the reason they had become friends in the first place. William himself had been curious about the expedition around *Mem* and what the three men had discovered although he knew nothing about his personality change. As he was remembering those earlier days, he realized that he really knew very little about what she was talking about. But, thinking that it might be important to her he said, "Well, I can share something of interest that happened to us when we were out on an assignment in *Yurland*. Warren was the lead and I was just along for the ride, so to speak. I probably wasn't even supposed to be there. I wasn't a detective quite yet. We were on a stakeout and he mentioned a trip he had made sometime before into central *Weeklun* and meeting someone there that had changed his life. Those were almost the very words he used. I'm sorry to say I never asked him for any more details. I thought he would tell me if he wanted to. At the time it seemed more of a passing comment than anything else.

"You said you didn't know him before?" she asked. "I need to be sure of that."

William shook his head; he knew what she was driving at. "To me he's always been the happy-go-lucky guy he's always been as far as I know. It was his positive attitude about everything that was one of the things that I liked about him even when we were in serious scrapes together."

She didn't want to hear about those serious scrapes. They would only add to her burden of memories of him. She could ask later if need be. She went on. "I think that his change had something to do with the missing time and memory we all face," she replied.

He was studying the tablecloth as she said this. After a long pause he replied, "That's an odd idea. What would make you think that?""

Her face was serious, her voice calm and almost quiet. “Something else happened after he got back from that trip. I’ve never told anyone else about it. As you might imagine I knew very exactly when his time of oblivion, that’s what he used to call it, would start and end each time that it happened. You can’t live with someone for as many years as we had without noticing such things. Well, I can still remember it clearly, it was a Monday several weeks after he had returned home. Monday was his day you know. I was working in the kitchen.”

Wini paused and then added, “I’m so glad that the police department is willing to shift work days so that detectives are able to take their day off on the same day as their time of oblivion.”

William smiled in agreement as he strained forward to hear what else she was going to tell him.

She went on, “It was around fifteen minutes after noon and the house was quiet. I assumed that he was back in our bedroom lying down during his time. It almost always lasted twenty-eight minutes or so. He often did this when he was home. The door was closed. But as I opened it quietly there, he was sitting in his easy chair reading, fully awake and responsive. He wasn’t comatose or out of touch as he usually was. I was really surprised because it was the first time, I had ever seen him acting normally when he should have been unresponsive or whatever state you want to call it. I know that he tried to cover it up as if nothing unusual was going on and I went on as if it wasn’t anything unusual either. We both played our parts well. But from then on, I wondered how he could have done it. Something had changed.”

William’s eyes were wide, his mouth open in surprise. “Maybe you mixed up the day of the week?” he finally offered.

“No, I’m certain it was his day and I’m sure the time

was correct too. I was really puzzled. As I said, I've never told anyone else about it."

"I'm sure."

"Well, it happened again almost a year later only this time he acted more ashamed or embarrassed than he had the other time. It was like he had gotten caught doing something he shouldn't have, like a little boy who gets caught stealing a cookie."

"So what happened?" he asked.

"Like before, it was a Monday around noon and we were planning to go out to do some shopping right after he had come out of his amnesia time. But earlier that same morning he had been acting differently toward me, like he was immensely proud or something. It was like he wanted me to recognize what it was. He came into the kitchen just after noon and sat down. He had a strange look on his face. I had the impression he wanted to tell me something. I wasn't noticing what time it was and he began telling me some more about his trip around *Memlandia.* Of course, he had done this before and each time he liked to add little details, probably to make it more interesting for me. I thought it was just because he was so proud of himself for completing it. Well, we both got so engrossed in his story that we forgot what time it was. When he finished it was twelve thirty-five! I didn't even realize that he hadn't slipped into his memnesia time until later that day. I don't know if he realized it or not either. Later I began to think that he was really trying to show me that he had overcome his time of memory loss somehow, but we both just overlooked it and went on with the rest of the day. But I can tell you I never forgot it, William. You know I had the strangest feeling that he had done it deliberately."

The young man was deep in thought trying to put one and one together with what he knew about the man he had shared police duty with for all those years. What

Wini had just told him brought to mind things that Warren had shared with him when they were on long boring stakeouts together. Her news opened his eyes to new possibilities that had suddenly taken on tremendous consequences; many questions flashed through his mind, "What if he had stumbled onto the key of *Mem's* curse? What if the accident that killed him wasn't an accident at all? Who else might have known about Warren's secret and were they trying to get control of it? How can I find out? There had to be a connection here someplace." He was deep in thought when Wini broke in again.

"I've got to tell you something else, William. You're not to disclose it to anyone."

He nodded in agreement even though he didn't know what she was about to tell him.

"Last night as I was falling to sleep-I've not slept well at all since he died-I think he spoke to me."

He studied her face and saw a woman deeply distraught and questioning inside; lines of worry and sadness mingled there amid her tears; she started to cry silently again. At length he said, "Wini, you've been through so much. Are you sure you want to tell me about it?"

"Yes. I've got to tell someone. It's so unreal, so impossible to believe." She stopped to wipe her eyes and cheeks with a tissue before going on. "You see, it was his voice. I'm sure of it. And he spoke to me so gently." She began to cry again.

"What did he say?"

She bowed her head and breathed deeply trying to get up the courage to tell him everything. She finally answered, "William, he told me where he had hidden a little book that he received from that old man he had met. At first, I didn't understand what he was talking about. Then the pieces came together. I think it was what he had been carrying inside himself for all these years, what a burden it must have been. In my dream, if it was a dream, I realized what a terrible wife I'd been for not trusting or understanding him as I should have."

William's heart raced, his breathing deepened and quickened, his face flushed. While he didn't necessarily believe that Warren had spoken to her from the grave, he still had to find out what he had said to her. "Wini, please, this is really important. I want you to go back and tell me everything he said. I'll keep your secret. No one else will know its source."

"All right," she replied, "it was after midnight and I was having trouble getting to sleep as usual. Ever since his death every time I closed my eyes, I could see him driving home from work in the dark and then that sudden head-on collision. Every time it's almost like I was there too. I tried to sleep with my eyes open. Finally, I calmed down and tried to think about something pleasant. Sometime after that I thought I heard his voice. It wasn't spooky or anything, not like it was coming down a tunnel or anything but just his musical friendly voice, you know."

"Yes, yes, and what did he say?"

"Well what I remember is that he said the book of secrets is in a file. That's what he called it, the book of secrets. Whatever that means. That's all I can really remember. He didn't say my name but I knew it was him." She continued to sob quietly.

William grew even more excited although he was certain that no one else would believe that the source of this information, a voice in a dream, was reliable. He had to accept it only as possibly corroborative evidence, evidence that would never be admissible in any court of law. He took her trembling hand gently in his and looked into her wet eyes and said, "Wini, thank you for sharing this secret with me. I won't break your trust."

After some more minutes of small talk she said,

"Well, William, it looks like we're not much farther along than we were before. What do you think we should do next?" Her eyes were still damp as she looked down at the intricate pattern of her carpet without seeing it.

He thought for a while and suddenly brightened, "It probably won't lead anywhere but I can read through his official police file, at least the non-confidential sections and see if he might have left some clues or something. Maybe they are the files he was referring to."

"That's a great idea. Will you tell me if you find anything?" she asked with new excitement.

"According to protocol I'll have to clear it with the chief first," he said. "You understand."

"Of course, I do. I hope you'll uncover something there. And I'll look around the house. Maybe he left something here." Her voice wasn't as depressed as before.

As he stood up to leave, he wondered if his visit had only served to open up new wounds; he noticed the anxiety that still clung to her like a heavy shroud. He could tell she was still deeply troubled about something. He didn't know what it was and didn't want to probe. He said, "I think it's probably time for me to go. I hope our meeting was productive for you. I know it has been for me. Let's stay in close touch."

Then, without any preamble or explanation at all Wini said almost in a whisper, "I was starting to work on my exit plan."

He looked at her with alarm. He didn't know if he had heard her correctly or what she was talking about; he was afraid to ask. "Was she talking about suicide? Had she somehow learned something else from Warren that she hadn't told him?" Finally, he decided to let it drop so that their long silent hug might fill the void as he left.

3

William's Research

Memnesia was so old and familiar, so taken for granted, that modern-day scientists had virtually given up studying it. It was viewed simply as a variation of normal sleep and garnered only minor attention within the scientific community-most of whom worked in academia and pursued quite independent or at least tangential subjects. Nevertheless, after he had heard what Wini had told him William became obsessed with this periodic loss of time and memory that every *Memlandian* faced. The more he thought about Warren's behavior and what Wini had told him the more convinced he was that somehow Warren had learned some secret of Mem and had actually been practicing it.

He surprised himself when he discovered that he had a natural talent for research. He sorted his basic lists of questions into logical groups of inquiries and formed hypotheses that he could test. He also read what was known about the differences and similarities between short- and long-term memory and whether *Memnesia* might simply be a variation of one of them. He deduced quickly that it could not because of its precise time of onset each day for all *Daytunians*, once each week for *Weeklundians* and once a year for *Yurlundians.* Then he looked into the question of whether forgetting at other times of the day or night is really the same thing as noontime memnesia? This was a particularly crucial question since he realized that in order to forget something one had to have something in memory in the first place whereas *Memnesia* seemed to him more of a partial system shutdown like a failure of encoding, storage, or retrieval of information.

William spent lots of his free time on university campuses in their libraries and talking with several professors. They told him that laboratory research had discovered that memory acted to allow people to adapt more quickly to changes in the environment, that is, it played a valuable survival role for *Memlandians.* The main idea was that the contents in one's memory acts as a valve or filter that continually assesses the risk-to-reward ratio of doing one thing over another. William had to drop this idea, however, because there was no memory at all during periods of *Memnesia.* This could only put people in greater danger not less.

He also learned from a noted neurobiologist that stronger and longer lasting memories come from deeper and more primitive parts of a *Memlandian's* central nervous system. He had suggested that this pointed to a very early origin for their memory dysfunction, MD as some called it. Yet even if this were true it couldn't help him understand the impact of *Memnesia* today.

Since people could remember things accurately that occurred before and soon after the MD period, but not during it, both input and encoding of things were probably not the main contributors to it. Their neurological connections were still functioning before and after the MD period. He reasoned that this left the retrieval mechanism as the primary culprit. Something was happening in the brains of *Memlandians* during their MD that blocked the extraction of information. He also learned that competition for attention, a form of system overload, did not prevent the formation of a memory in the first place. Finally, William discovered that the kind of sensory experiences involved in one's memory of past events doesn't play any major role in MD either. *Memnesia* simply blocked all senses, all consciousness.

Over the next several weeks William began to form his own hypothesis of how memory dysfunction worked. He reasoned that it must involve a disruption of the brain's inherent neuronal connections along with their hormonal control or receptivity. His was clearly a naturalistic approach based on firmly established scientific principles. It was all he knew.

. . .

As a detective in Morristown's police department William had authority to search its voluminous files in the basement without anyone's approval except Bob Rogers, his supervising captain. "I doubt he will object," he thought to himself, "particularly when he hears that the chief is also interested in what I might find out." Fifteen minutes later William had gotten his go-head and was headed down to the basement and the department's voluminous files.

William had starting working for the police department right out of college. His computer science courses and degree had helped him land the job in their data processing department. He knew the ins and outs of computer data files better than anyone except, perhaps, Warren who had been appointed chief administrative E and F (evidence and files) clerk soon after he joined the force. Then Warren had gone on to become a detective.

William checked in with Emmett Carlson who had been appointed to take over the E and F Department right after Warren's death. Emmett was a thin mild-mannered man with a nervous tick in his neck and pale complexion. He wasn't an athletic man at all; he seemed to be well-suited for a desk job. Emmett had quickly discovered what a masterful job Warren had done in organizing the department's written files as well as all of its physical evidence. He looked up at William standing in front of his desk and asked, "So detective, how can I help you?"

William introduced himself and then replied, "I need to see the official files on Warren Wheaton... after he became a detective."

Emmett gave him a rapid sideways look as if to say, "What do you need those for?" But he knew enough not to ask. He had no authority to do any more than to check and write down his badge number, retrieve whatever files William wanted, and get the date, time and his initials on his form. He would record their return later.

William quickly added, "I was his partner."

This news brought a broad smile of understanding to Emmett's face. "Just a minute and I'll go get them for you," he said.

"Oh, don't bother. Just tell me where they are and I'll save you the trip," William replied.

Emmett paused a second. "Well, I'm not supposed to let anyone into that section of the files but for you, I guess I don't see anything wrong." He smiled again, glad to be helping the partner of a famous predecessor. "Go on, you'll find the first one in aisle D, file box 6117 according to my computer here."

"Great." William found the file box quickly, thanks to the numbering and labelling system Warren had developed long before. He pulled the heavy box off the shelf, signed for it, and carried it to one of the three small private carrels to go through it. If he needed to take the box outside the files department he would need two more signatures which he didn't have and wasn't going to get unless it was absolutely necessary.

William approached his search of Warren's files as if he was carrying out an official case investigation. Of course he wasn't.

. . .

Unbeknownst to everyone Warren had been very careful to record only factual information in his own police files, the kind of information that might be needed and admissible in a court of law someday. Yet as William searched deeper in the many file folders, he noticed Warren's clever way of obscuring certain facts while emphasizing others. Information that he thought was important enough to need obscuring could have been encrypted in one way or another yet Warren knew that using text encryption would make these details immediately suspect and a focus of even greater attention so he found other ways to bury them in plain sight; he buried them amid innocuous sentences or paragraphs that, while the whole text still made sense, the details he needed to make disappear were not readily noticed. These were the typed and hand-written files that William was scanning rapidly.

. . .

"Well, he sure was compulsive," he thought as he slowly and carefully read through the three page-long subject index, the chronology Warren had prepared for his entire file, "Here's everything laid out for me... thanks Warren," he whispered to himself as he quickly scanned the short and concise paragraph abstracts that summarized each of the cases in which he had taken part. William didn't really know what he was looking for but hoped he would stumble onto some hint or even a "deliberate" mistake. After an hour he had progressed through the entire file and hadn't found anything of interest. "I need a break," he thought, and stood up to stretch. Then he got an idea.

"I can't find what I'm looking for," he said to the short partly-balding middle-aged man at the front desk. Maybe you can help me."

"Well, I don't know but I sure can try," Emmett replied with a smile. "Now what are you looking for?"

"Do you have a cross-file on particular cases that have been closed either because they went to court or were dropped?" he asked.

"Of course, I do." Which case are you interested in?" he asked.

"Well, I don't know how to identify it by name, date, type, number or defendant or much of anything else. The only thing I'm sure of is that Warren Wheaton was involved."

Emmett gave him an odd sort of look and shook his head. Then he said, "Well, young man that doesn't give me very much to work with does it?"

William shook his head in agreement as he replied in a lowered voice, "I guess not. Does your computer index give the name all the detectives and staff related to each closed case?

Emmett shook his head again.

"I was afraid of that. But, the date of the case I'm looking for was about ten or eleven years ago when Mr. Wheaton was on an official expedition going around *Mem* and...".

Emmett broke in, "Oh, I know which case that was 'cause back then, I was still in college, I was really interested in why our police department was involved in it. Let me think now; I think it was called something like Round-*Memland* Trip or something like that. As I recall it was funded by all three countries and had one man on it from each of them."

"Yes, that's it," William cried. "But I don't think he was a detective yet, Mr. Carlson. Would that make a difference?"

"No, I don't think so, just as long as he was a staff employee," he said.

William said, "You really have a great memory. Now, can you remember where that old file is?"

"I'll just check the computerized database he worked on and see if I can find out." He typed in several search terms and hit return. Almost instantaneously he had located the files. "There we are! I've got three for you," he cried, obviously proud of himself. The first is labelled *"Departmental Overview-Publicity Benefits of Participating in Official Round-Mem Expedition,"* the second is titled "*Close-out Summary-Official Round-Memland Expedition.*" The third seems to be some kind of cross-referenced paper. It's called "*The Etiology of Memory Loss.*" He perked up even more as he shuffled back into his tall forest of metal shelves that held hundreds and hundreds of large cardboard file boxes; he brought out a heavy cardboard box and set it on the counter. He said, "Well, detective here's the first one. I can't let you check out more than one box at a time. You'll have to sign out for each one separately, that's regulations. It's better to do one at a time anyway. That way things don't get mixed up. I'll leave the others where they are for when you need them."

William quickly signed out for the first box. It wasn't as heavy as he had expected. He was getting excited now; the detective in him sensed he would surely discover some clue here. It was only after another hour and forty-five minutes, however, that he put the last papers back in the first box and sighed. "Nothing important here that I can see. It's all about the publicity the department would gain by having one of their own taking part. Maybe I went too fast and missed something." Rather than reread the file over again, however, he decided to read through the second box that was supposed to describe the official findings of the international expedition that the department considered important enough to record for posterity. William turned in the first box and signed out the second.

He wasn't surprised to learn that they had expected Warren to write most of the report since he had been the source of the greater part of its information. Almost an hour had gone by and William was only half-way through its stack of neatly typed and numbered pages when he spotted two sentences Warren had written. They seemed to have been embedded within a longer paragraph:

> *"I remember talking to an old man during my trip through central Weeklun. The old man claimed some special, rather esoteric knowledge but, since the meeting did not appear relevant to the subject at hand, I sought no further information from or about him. cross reference The Etiology of Memory Loss, pg. 38."*

William also noticed that the date was June 4th. He paused when he read these words and wondered if that old man might have been the same person Warren, and now Wini, had recently mentioned to him? "He had to be. What could be the chance there were two on a trip like that?" he reasoned. Now he was really getting excited for here was actual written evidence of that meeting somewhere in central *Weeklun*. He knew he was onto something. It was the first tangible clue he had uncovered. He was glad that Warren had been both honest and compulsive enough to write it down in his official trip report. He would tell Wini about it the next time they met. Nevertheless, William also wondered why Warren hadn't mentioned that old man anywhere else in his own personal file, the one he had read earlier in the day. The only possible reference there had been two words "*wondrous contact on June 4th*". "Did he leave him out on purpose?" he asked himself. Suddenly he remembered that the dates were the same. It had been the same man! He decided to go back and reread Warren's file again, this time much more carefully.

William made a note of the location of this new information, carried the file box back to Emmett, signed it back in again, and checked out the box labelled, Wheaton, Warren.

It was more than an hour later that William, now skimming line-by-line, found an obscure note written in the margin that said, "to *Misc – Closed Cases.*" It was in Warren's handwriting. The words didn't relate to the preceding text and seemed to be out of place. "Why would he write something like that?" he asked himself. It was a clue and he was a detective; the two realities merged together easily and became entwined; he couldn't get those words out of his mind. He went back to Emmett's desk.

"What? Back again young man? One would have thought you could track down your suspect or evidence or whatever faster than that." He said this with a smile that made his words nearly unoffensive.

"Well, you've got to admit that I may be a fairly new detective but I am tenacious. Now, I'm looking for a file labelled *"Misc – Closed Cases."* He said this as he handed the Wheaton file back a second time. He watched with anticipation as the chief file clerk typed in the words on his keyboard and then smiled with the look of a general who knew he was about to win a battle. Then he shuffled back into his files yet again without a word.

As he vanished down an aisle he muttered under his breath, "Do you really know what you're looking for? Wait 'til you see all the files there are with that title." He made the trip over and over again until he had loaded nine large file boxes on his roller sled. The bearings of its wheels were worn and squeaked as he pushed them back toward the front desk. "Are you sure you want all of them?" he asked with a quizzical look. In all of the time he has served as the Chief of the files and evidence department he had never had a detective request so many boxes.

William stared at the tottering stack and gulped. He wasn't sure whether he really wanted to spend the next several days going through them all. He asked, "Is there any way to check them out by date or anything else? I'm pretty sure Warren would have cross-coded them."

Mr. Carlson thought for a moment before replying. "Well sir. I've never had anyone request all these files at the same time before and I really don't know. So, I guess I owe you some congratulations, you're the first. But you'll still have to check out one box at a time to see if you can find what you're looking for."

William looked at his watch. It was already four p.m. and he didn't feel like attacking this new pile today. "I'm pretty much out of time today," he said, "I'll have to come back again sometime soon. Can you leave these files out for me?"

"Young man. You don't understand about keeping track of files, do you? If I started doing that, I would not only lose control of the whole system but probably lose my job as well." He made it clear that he was more than annoyed by having to return them all. "I'll put them back for you now but I'll also drape a small red ribbon over the front of each one to save me time next time you come in asking for them." He didn't grin as he muttered this. Yet still, he was proud of himself for having come up with such a clever solution as this. As William left his office, he jotted down his exit time and badge number – 2446.

On his way back to his own office William stopped by the chiefs'. "Chief, I just wanted you to know that I've spent most of the day in files... Warren's case. I went through a lot of reports and supporting material but I found nothing very important on what we're looking for except that Warren met an old man in the forest during his Round-*Memland* expedition, but you knew that already. But I do have another possible lead to follow-up on the next time I'm in files."

"Well, detective," the chief began, "what do you mean by 'the next time you're in files'?" Are you going to go fishing in the meantime? I'd suggest you get on with it, bright and early tomorrow morning!"

"Yes sir," was the only reply he could give his superior as he turned and left his office with a sheepish look plastered on his face. He was glad none of the other detectives had see him.

. . .

Meanwhile, Wini had just dialed Danielle to return her call and see how she was doing. "Hello Danielle, this is Wini. I just wanted to call to say hi and say thanks for your call the other day. How are you two doing?"

"What a surprise! It's so good to hear from you. We're fine. Did you know that Duncan got a new job? He's not driving a delivery truck anymore. With his Master's Degree he's found a part-time teaching position at a Jr. College. He's a professor now and he loves it! Would you believe it?" She was so proud she almost shouted the news.

"Oh, I'm so very glad for you Danielle. He surely deserves it as I remember from our time together at Compole Inn... you remember, we had such a fun time."

Danielle had read about Warren's tragic death in the papers and had deliberately waited to call Wini. Her earlier call had only been to make sure that she didn't need anything. She knew Wini needed time to grieve and settle down. After a pause she said, "Wini, remember when Yvonne shared with us that she thought their marriage was on the rocks and then Yates walked up and kissed her and twirled her around in front of everybody around the pool? Wasn't that a wonderful change for them both." Danielle hoped this memory would help cheer Wini up. She went on, "Duncan never did tell me what had happened to change Yate's personality like that."

"Of course I remember. That's not the kind of thing one could ever forget. You know it's interesting you mentioned that because Warren never told me either," she said as she began to smile to herself. "Even though I never commented about it at the time his abrupt change somehow reminded me a little of my Warren's change. The two seemed similar. But now...", Wini became quiet again as her new reality settled over her once again.

Danielle didn't know what she was talking about and didn't ask. However, she did say, "Wini, let's get together soon. It would be good to talk face-to-face, not over the phone. OK?"

They agreed to meet in another week after things calmed down at the Wheaton house.

. . .

William walked into the files department at seven thirty the next morning, a Saturday. It was breath-takingly cold outside and also in. The damp chill had permeated the poorly heated building throughout the night. William was glad he had brought his heavy coat.

While the F & E door was standing wide open no one was there. "He probably wanted to let some of the warmer air from the hallway get in, but that's really odd," he thought. "The evidence locker is wide open for anyone to come in and "borrow" whatever they might want. I'll bet there's a lot of very high value things back there."

During his job transition as a detective the Chief of Forensics had given him a list of procedural steps he was required to follow to keep any criminal evidence he came across both uncontaminated and correctly labelled. These two steps had been firmly emphasized. It had been made very clear to him that if either one were overlooked it could jeopardize the acceptability of the evidence in court. An opposing attorney could tear the case apart because the provenance of the evidence hadn't been kept accurate or secure at all times. And now, here, the whole evidence locker was standing wide open and unguarded. It didn't make any sense.

William was just about to phone the chief about it when he heard footsteps approaching in the hallway. It was Emmett carrying a cup of hot coffee in one hand and a donut in the other. He couldn't talk because he had a second donut in his mouth. He was startled when he saw William and spilled some coffee on the floor.

As he set everything down and took the powdered sugar donut out of his mouth he said, "Well, I didn't expect to find you or anyone else here at this time of day, especially on a Saturday." The white ring of powdered sugar on his lips made him look even older than he was.

"Obviously, but you should have locked the door when you left shouldn't you? I've heard it said that you're guarding a veritable gold mine of evidence down here."

The older man shook his head and replied, "Well, detective, if I'd done that how could I unlock and open the door with these in both hands?" He nodded downward toward his breakfast with an air of someone who had just beat another in a debate involving common sense and legalistic logic. A cup of hot coffee and donuts always beat police regulations!

William decided it was best to drop the matter. "I'm here to go through those files you so carefully marked with red ribbons yesterday."

"Yes sir," he replied and disappeared yet again into a nearby aisle. Several minutes later William heard the squeaking wheels of the cart before he saw them. It was piled high with brown cardboard filing boxes. Each had a red ribbon along with a typed label attached to its front side. Emmett said, "You know that you've got to check them out one at time... department regulations."

William replied, "All right, if you insist," and signed for the first box.

William carried the box to the table where he had been working and checked its label. It listed the Case Closure Date, Number, and name of the Chief Detective or Supervising Administrative Official of each case. He realized that this information wouldn't be much help in finding what he was looking for. "I guess I'll just have to slog through the whole box," he thought with a sense of failure even before he had even begun.

Inside he found a piece of paper lying on top of all of the files. As he ran his finger down the list of the four-teen cases he found the names of all participants in each case along with a short paragraph summary of what had happened. "Thanks again, buddy," he mumbled quietly to himself. He quickly searched for Warren's name. It wasn't listed in box 1 or in any of the next six boxes.

It was almost four hours later that he finally saw Warren Wheaton's name along with others in the summary of the contents of one of the last cases stored in the seventh box; the case was an investigation of a sting operation. William's heart began to beat faster as he read the case details.

> *"Location: North-Central Weeklun, 12 miles W of Readsville. Stake-out on 3-6-04 through 3-10-04 by (H.R.-2219, T.S.-2422, W.W.-2445)*

He didn't need to read any farther since neither the date nor location fit. He sighed as he replaced the file and went to get the next box, number eight. For some reason it was lighter than the others had been. He lifted its lid and read the contents typed meticulously on the cover sheet. He immediately found Warren's name on three of the nine cases in side. Two of them were relatively current but it was clear that the third was the one he was looking for. Its date corresponded with the date of the "Round-*Memland* Expedition." "Yes! I've found it," he exclaimed out loud.

"That's great Mr. Thomas. You didn't take as long as I thought you would." Emmett's voice came from down the hall.

William didn't reply. He began to read the case file slowly and carefully. He learned that Warren had been temporarily reassigned from being head of the files department in order to act as an undercover agent who would take part in the official police assignment (the report didn't mention that Warren had applied for the expedition well before his subsequent official approval). Although the police department needed a participant who was not only qualified to take part in the expedition but who would not be suspected of being on official assignment his appointment also had been approved by officials high up in *Weeklun's* civilian government.

William's respect for him grew even more.

Warren's two travelling companions were Dave Morris, 27, of *Daytun* who held a Masters degree in Biology and considered to be a highly promising researcher, and Dr. Yeiren Yarom, 39, a professor of physics at *Yurland's* largest university. William jotted down their names, affiliations and addresses in case he might need to contact them. Their assignment had been to find out whether time varied anyplace on *Mem* (it was thought at the time that the rate at which time passed might differ around the planet and perhaps explain the different lengths of amnesia found in each country). But Warren's actual mission had been covert. He was supposed to try to search for any evidence of smuggling activities.

The now officially closed case file of this assignment described many other interesting things but nothing appeared to be important to William until he came to something buried within a much longer paragraph. It briefly summarized a side-trip Warren had taken one day. It looked to William as if Warren had tried to bury the text by not indenting or otherwise bringing attention to it. He had written: Date: June 9th; Day 34. "Departed 6:00 a.m. from camp (location: latitude: approx. 98 miles south of Compole; longitude: approx. four days travel W. of *Daytun/ Weeklun* boundary). Due south from there alone for seven hrs. Met old man (J.C.) for twelve wonderful hrs."

Warren had underlined the word wonderful for some reason.

William was thrilled at finding this new piece of information that Warren had cleverly concealed in his report. Others would probably overlook it as nothing important. It was another piece of the puzzle that gave him more valuable information about where the old man had lived. He was certain that he was the same person that Wini had told him about. But was there anything more? He kept reading.

He was impressed with his friend's gift for writing. It was clear and yet cryptic; in a way it read like something in a spy novel. William read that they discovered that time did not vary because of geographic location. Warren had typed the following in italics:

> *"According to our measurements (and within reasonable limits of equipment error) the amnesia everyone on Mem experiences cannot have been caused by some small deviation(s) of local time."*

He also discovered in a separate hand-written footnote that Warren had added months later, that the same measurements had been repeated by a second team and that they had found the same thing.

When he had finished digesting the field report William knew that he should also read Warren's daily log-book from that trip. Perhaps he would find something of importance there as well.

It was eleven forty-five when he finally finished reading the main case file. He decided he would read Warren's personal trip logbook after lunch. While the chief had been pretty clear about him not putting off to tomorrow what he should do today his stomach was beginning to make it quite clear that lunch was important too. William would come back and finish the job then. He thought that he had already hit pay dirt and there probably would be little more to find.

William had been so focused in his search that he had forgotten what day it was. Three minutes before both hands of his watch reached twelve William felt the familiar symptoms that would make him a prisoner of noon once again. He quickly sat down in his carrel and pretended to be reading if someone had been watching. Fortunately, there was no one else there except Mr. Carlson. While his spells were no secret-everyone had them-somehow, he still felt intimidated and secretly embarrassed by them. "They're a sign of weakness that detectives shouldn't have," he thought.

Five minutes later Mr. Carlson called out, "Say there, detective Thomas, I've got to lock up for lunch now." He got no reply so he said again, "Did you hear me? You'll have to leave until twelve forty-five. You can continue your work then." Still he heard nothing. He began to worry what had happened and got up to find out. He walked back to William's carrel where he found him comatose and totally unresponsive. Although he was sure he knew why William was unconscious he had no idea how long it would last until he checked his MD wrist bracelet. "I can't lock up with someone inside, not for that long, detective or not," he thought to himself. He was frustrated that he would have to stay and miss his lunch but glad that he was a *Weeklundian.*

William returned to his normal consciousness at fourteen past noon. He was relieved that it happened faster than it did for most others. His hearing returned first and then his sight. Finally, he remembered where he was and what he was doing. He stretched his arms up over his head and gave a loud yawn that got Mr. Carlson's attention.

"Are you all right?" he called out.

"Are you talking to me?" William replied, still groggy.

"Yes, are you OK?"

William detected curtness in his voice. He replied, "Yes, I'm fine."

"Well detective I'm hungry and I need to go to lunch."

William was perplexed. He didn't know why Mr. Carlson would say something like that, however he didn't respond.

Both men remained quiet for several more minutes until Carlson blurted out, "I've got to lock up for lunch now. You've got to leave. You can come back at one-fifteen if you want to." (Emmett was going to get all the lunch period he was entitled to).

"Yes, of course," William replied as he arranged everything on the desk, stood up and finally left the files room. As he passed Emmett he had no idea why he received such a strange look. "I'll be back later," was all he said.

It was a cool, windy Autumn day with the sun already hanging low above the horizon. Leaves and papers swirled around the street and sidewalk. After his morning session in files William needed some fresh air; he set out for a brisk exercise walk until one o'clock.

He had only gone a little over a block from the police station and was crossing the street when it happened. Suddenly he heard the rapidly growing sound of a vehicle speeding toward him from behind. It seemed to come out of nowhere; he hadn't noticed hardly any traffic before. He turned around just in time to see the huge dark blur of a pick-up truck heading straight for him. It was only because of his youthful reflexes and athletic coordination that he was able to jump backward onto the sidewalk at the last second; the truck sideswiped the curb nearby leaving only its black tire marks, a rising cloud of leaves and a rush of air against his body. It had missed him by only a foot or two at the most. He looked up in surprise because the driver kept right on going!

William wasn't able to get his license number only its color and body style. He sat down on the sidewalk for a while in partial shock. He had almost been killed. "Was it only an accident or deliberate? I never even saw him coming. Who would want to do something like that to me?" he thought. He couldn't find any immediate answers.

He was still in shock and out of breath when he got back to the station; he reported the "near" hit and run to the desk sergeant who took down what little information there was and gave the young detective a look as if to say, "You've got to be kidding, reporting something like that. I've got more important things to do."

William thought it was his duty to report it.

Finally returning to the files room just after the required return time and a little shaken up he asked Emmett to get him the file box containing Warren's daily trip diary from his Around-*Mem* Expedition. Emmett checked his computer again, looked up and said, "It's supposed to be in box 8. Isn't it there?"

William checked the file box again and finally found it lying flat-out of sight on the bottom. "Yeh, it's here. I missed it before," he called out. When he looked over at Emmett it was clear something was wrong. Emmett had a sour look on his face (he had been late at his favorite restaurant and they had run out of the entre he had been looking forward to). William could also tell that he'd been drinking. Emmett tried to cover up his slightly slurred speech and steadied himself with both hands on his desk.

William took the diary out and, holding it upside down, fanned its worn stained pages to see if any separate pieces of paper might fall out. None did. Then he checked for a subject index in the front that might save him time in locating what he was looking for. There was no index either. William had no choice. He had to read the entire one hundred forty-six pages of tiny, neatly lettered pages of text and hope that something important would jump out at him.

It was three-forty p.m. when he finally found it, the original notation for the event he had read earlier in the official case file. There in Warren's own neat hand writing was:

"Day 34, 6/9/; Departed alone 6:00 a.m. from camp at lat. approx. 98 miles south of Compole; long. approx. four days travel W. from Daytun/ Weeklun border. Due south-six hrs. on foot. Met with Mr. J. Clemmans for 13 hrs. Learned much

William noticed the last two underlined words and wondered what they meant. He also saw that a page had been torn out of the notebook after this one and that Warren had left out perhaps the most important fact of all in his official typed report, the name of his contact-J. Clemmans!

As significantly, William noticed that all of the following entries were clearly different. Warren's cursive hand writing seemed more excited and irregular in some way. Entries were worded more positively and included many more adjectives of joy and gratitude with far less negativity than those before. He was fascinated as he noticed the abrupt change in how Warren had described his daily experiences, including his weekly periods of amnesia. Warren had praised someone with the initials Y.Y. for his willingness to help D.N. with his daily loss of memory. At first William didn't know what they referred to until he reread the beginning of the trip notes and discovered the initials referred to his two travelling companions.

William had never enjoyed his own memory dysfunction that took control over him each week. He never said, "I want to forget that!" as he might have after experiencing some trauma. But as he continued to read Warren's trip diary notes he came across the following in a very tiny, hand-written text:

"J.C. told me that it is so ancient and ingrained that it has become accepted as part of our proud heritage, our very life. For those who will not learn it is a wound that never fully heals."

Now William knew who J.C. was and guessed that "it" referred to the amnesia everyone faced. His brain whirled at what he was reading; did it blur meaning and conceal some greater truth or make things clearer? Or was it all a lie? He was confused by these clues to a mystery that he felt increasingly driven to solve.

"Who are those who will not learn?" he thought. Was Warren talking about himself?

He finally finished reading Warren's day log at four forty-five in the afternoon. He was tired but excited at the same time. All that small cursive hand writing had strained his eyes and he needed a rest. He made a few more notes and then turned box eight containing Warren's log book in to Emmett and said, "Well, I think one more session should do it... only one more file box to go through. It's been quite a day" (He didn't tell Mr. Carlson about almost being run down at lunch time). "I'm through for the day," he said out loud.

By now Mr. Carlson had mostly recovered from his delayed liquid refreshment at lunch and was able to smile again. He replied, "All right, I've got to lock up at five anyway unless you have the chief's authorization to work late."

"No, I don't. I'll see you tomorrow morning."

Emmett gave him a strange look, closed one eye, and cocked his head to one side as he replied, "Are you sure, sir? It's Sunday. And by the way, thanks for today. I was working overtime." (He didn't mention that the chief had called him to make sure he would come in on Saturday to assist William).

William felt embarrassed. He had been so involved in his research that he had forgotten what day it was. He also had no remembrance of his loss of time at noon. It was as if nothing at all untoward had happened even though Emmett knew the truth. William replied, "Oh, so it is, sorry. It'll have to be Monday then," and he left for home to give Granville his evening treat and try to relax a little.

. . .

Wini had tried to stay busy during those first few weeks after he died. She took long walks by herself in a nearby park and tried to read a novel that she had set aside for months. She gave up after the first few pages. She started to telephone several girl-friends hopefully for some long chats-but hung up without connecting with any of them because she really didn't want to have to go through the same painful: “Yes, I’m OK, thanks... No. I don’t need anything, thanks.” She also spent time in her kitchen trying out new recipes until one day she got around to calling her boss at the paper.

“Hello Jim? This is Wini. Do you have a minute?”

“Of course, I do Wini. I’ve been thinking of you. Please, take all the time you want,” he replied.

“Jim, first of all, I’m OK. It’ll take some time but I think things will calm down and I can come back in to work. In fact, I think it probably would be good for me. It would take my mind off what happened,” she began. “I’ve been going through my memories with him, all those good times, and I miss him more than ever.”

He was nodding although she couldn’t see it. He said, “Well, I think that’s a wise thing to do. Step back for a while and let things settle down. Is there something I can do for you right now Wini? You must have called for a reason.”

She paused for a moment before replying. She really hadn’t called him with any request more, perhaps, than just to hear a familiar voice, a touch with the past. But she answered, “Jim, I do appreciate your support. I guess I just wanted to tell you that.”

“Wini. You’re a very special person to me... to all of us here at the paper. We all wish you the best, you know that. If there’s ever anything we can do don’t hesitate to get in touch, OK? And we’re really looking forward to when you can come back to work. You’re a top-notch reporter.”

Wini started to tear-up, her voice began to break and she didn’t want to show it. She remained silent for a while.

“Wini? Are you still there?” he finally asked.

She had been distracted for as he was talking a

string of thoughts suddenly had entered her mind out of nowhere. She didn't tell him about them. "Maybe I can find out what happened to change Warren's personality. We were married for over a year before he changed so I'm sure the difference was real. I don't see any reason why he would make it up. He never was very good at acting," she thought rapidly to herself. Maybe he left something here at home that I've overlooked."

"Yes Jim... I'm... still here. When that time comes, you'll be the first to know. Good bye Jim, and thanks."

"Good bye."

They both hung up.

Then Wini began her own personal search for evidence-but evidence of what? She began by cleaning out his dresser drawers. She justified what she was doing by donating his suits, shoes, rain coat, and other clothing to the local goodwill. She threw out all his socks. "They'll like all of these things I'm sure," she mumbled to herself as she set his clothes on the bed in neat piles. She paused holding Warren' favorite wool sweater to her face and smelled the traces of his body that remained in the yarn. Then she broke down and cried. "Oh, how I miss you so."

She finished her culling through his dresser in less than an hour. As she was finishing the bottom drawer, she noticed a white envelope that he had taped out of sight on the rear side. "Why would he do that?" she asked herself. Then she understood. He had done it deliberately so she would only find it if she were cleaning everything out, like she was doing now.

She carefully removed it and sat on the edge of the bed nearby. She was trembling for she knew it would be important. She found her reading glasses and then slowly peeled it open. Inside were several sheets of paper; the first was written in his own hand. The words blurred in her tear-filled eyes.

She wiped them again and read his note:

Dearest Wini,

If I should die before you here is something that you must read. I share these words with you because they reflect the wisdom that came to me from a meeting I had with a very wise man during my participation on the *Round-Mem-Expedition* that you will remember.

I know that what I type here may not make much sense to you now but in time it will.

Please keep them safe and share them only with those you can trust.

I love you so much,

War

What followed were several typed pages. She tried to picture the two of them talking and what the other man had looked like, how he talked, why he had told Warren these things? She knew she should read them:

We have lost so much time and for what? Although it is so fundamental, so foundational to everything that exists on Mem it still hides from us now, like a camouflaged, hidden jungle animal that is never caught, never tamed, and cannot be controlled. For us Memlandians, this jungle animal may not be invisible at all; it is we who are blind. And why do we show so much indifference and arrogance toward our loss? It's because we are unconsciously ignoring its Creator-who is our God.

Whatever time is it is far greater than any Memlandian. It cannot be tamed by any means for we continue to lose it minute by minute even while we might grasp for it. Wini, time is a primary attribute of the One who created it. These thoughts about this wondrous hidden jungle animal have filled my mind many times.

Could the shape of our prowling beast be that of a line, a two-dimensional creature with only a head and tail, a snake? Yet even a line drawn on paper need not be linear as time is. It can curve and cross-upon itself and even end where it begins. Can time be as unconstrained as this? The string theory of our ancients tried to force time into this wondrous complex mold without success.

And is time's unidirectionality due only to God's wise kindness or to something else? Is He actually showing His loving kindness for us on Mem by not permitting us to know what our future holds? Might God have some other hidden purpose in allowing time to flow out from Him in only one direction and not in reverse so that we might return to Him? Could this be yet another sign of His kindness, another reflection of God's nature? For whom among us wants to know the date or moment of his death? Yet mercifully, God has limited life span in order to limit the evil that we might do - it is truly wise that all despots must die eventually. And why has He given us brains with a memory for past events but not for visions of future ones? These questions are tiresome indeed.

And the jungle creature called time creeps on no matter how hard we try to guide his course, his speed, the inevitable consequences of his presence. We do this ignorantly, arrogantly, even piously until our own personal time runs out and the jungle animal finally leaves us... for another?

Indeed, time is so fundamental that it must be independent of all other known physical and mental elements.

And what if time isn't just passing us by as we Memlandians commonly think? What if it is being created continuously and expanding into cosmic space to fill the whole Universe and thereby increase manifold entropy even more? What if it isn't simply another second of time that has already existed and then suddenly appears sixty times every minute? What if it's an entirely brand-new, freshly created second made to fill the void that was created by the fleeing, disintegrating jungle animal?

And even if time, space and energy do comprise dimensions of God Himself that would not preclude Him from also existing beyond them. Some call this His extra-dimensional *<u>Omni</u>presence and <u>Omni</u>potence. Where is God right now? Some call this place 'heaven' which is clearly a spatial word. Others call it 'eternity,' a temporal word. If both of these are true then it's likely that without God there can be neither time nor space. Can there be a Creation without a Creator? Can there be existence without time? Without them I cannot even exist to write these words.*

She thought, "What strange things to write. What was War trying to tell me? Maybe it wasn't written just to me, maybe someone else can make sense out of it."

She suddenly remembered William's keen interest as well and murmured out loud, "I'll show it to William and see if he thinks it's important." In the mean time she finished clearing out the things in his dresser and closet, packing them neatly and almost reverently in boxes for the goodwill store in town. She had no use for them anymore and hoped someone else would.

As she gently laid each item in place bits of Warren receded farther and farther from her.

It would take another day before this ritual was complete, before all the minute traces of the man she had lived with for all those years were finally uncovered and filed away in places that could not be retrieved even if she had wanted to. Each piece of clothing, each tool, each book he had enjoyed carried its own special memories. It was a terrible tearing task.

But other than the envelope hidden away in his bottom dresser drawer she found nothing else inside the house that was related to his round-*Mem* trip. She happened to notice that the rain parka he had taken on that trip wasn't in the bedroom closet. It was the forest-green, water-repellent one with lots of small pockets on the inside and outside.

It was approaching noon but due to her intense distractions she had forgotten about her own time of memnesia. She remembered that Warren's had occurred at noon on Mondays. Their difference in days of the week was one of the things they had seriously considered when they contemplated getting married. "This awful plague we all face, where did it come from? Why did everyone have to cope with it?" She had asked him many times in frustration.

Just then, Wini began to feel the unmistakable tingling in the soles of her feet. It signaled what was to come as surely as the morning's sun as it first peeked over the horizon to signal the certainty of the daylight hours. Its tingling was more temperate than electrical in nature; it was as if her feet had been immersed in a pan of ice-cold water. Over the next thirty seconds the same sensation rapidly rose up her spine to her shoulders and then it stopped for several long and suspenseful moments. She felt very chilled and was shivering. It had happened so many times before that she wasn't surprised-only anxious and frustrated at the loss of time she would have to waste. She knew that her mind was still working, so far. During the next stage the feeling changed to that of tiny pin pricks of electrical shock emanating from deep within her neck and spine that now travelled more slowly up to the top of her head- taking another half-minute to do so. That was the worst part of it for her. She hated this last slow torture, this expected awareness of what was coming next. At least it gave her mind time to get her body prepared. Every time it happened, she wondered whether everyone else in *Weeklun* went through the same thing. It was during this final pre-memnesia period that she tried to find a chair to sit in or a bed on which to lie. Otherwise she would merely collapse on the floor or the ground someplace and stay as still as death for about seventy-five minutes; this was somewhat longer than the average for her fellow *Weeklunders* yet far shorter than the longest period, which was a full day! When she had read these statistics in a government report years before she had thanked God that her episode was over so soon.

Wini quickly shuffled over to the bed, lay down, pulled up a light blanket over her and prayed. "Oh, dear God, here I go again. Please remember me even though I won't remember you. Please be kind to... " and then she became unconscious, once again.

Seventy-five minutes later she awoke, groggy and somewhat disoriented. As she lay there, she began to remember bits and snatches of what she had been doing before her MD. She had been searching through Warren's belongings. Anyway, she had to get rid of them sooner or later. She finally determined to get up and continue her unpleasant task.

She picked up each tie, each belt, each T shirt tenderly as if they were a part of Warren himself. And as she packed each thing she remembered some experience they had had together involving that item. She smelled each sweater again and again. He was there. Tears began streaming down her cheeks once more. Each tear reinforced the strength of her love for him.

The following day she rose early and forced herself to sort through things in his private domain, the garage. He had made the wall boards and shelves himself. They held all of his neatly arranged shop tools, his collection of airplane photographs that went back many decades, his collection of old history books and novels, and several other collections. She wondered what to do with them all.

She had hoped that he might have hidden something away in one of his books but she could find nothing. She was getting discouraged and frustrated at the same time. "Why am I wasting my time out here?" she asked herself. "There probably isn't anything else important anyway."

As she was going through a stack of old magazines she glanced across the garage and noticed Warren's all-weather green hiking jacket with its score of pockets. It was hanging limp on a nail. She was pretty sure that it was the one he had taken on his *Mem* hiking trip, as she had called it. Something made her go over and lift it off its nail. She methodically went through all of the outside pockets and found nothing except some stale peanuts, a candy bar wrapper, and some loose change. But when she went through its inside pockets, she found a sheet of paper folded into a small tight wad. It was as if he had wanted to be able to hide it easily.

Wini carried it over to his workbench and began to open it beneath one of the strong work-lights. Even without her reading glasses she could tell there were some numbers on one side; she didn't know what they stood for. She turned it over and opening the sheet further, smoothed its many fold lines on a clean flat surface. She made out printing in Warren's careful legible style; there was a single short paragraph! "I'd better go back inside and sit down to read this. Anyway, I need my glasses," she said out loud to no one.

She was getting excited now as she turned off the garage lights, locked the door, and sat down in her easy chair. "This could be something important. It's got to be from his trip around *Mem* long ago.

4

The Book of Secrets

Monday morning dawned with a constant light rain and cold mist. The cold outside penetrated into even the tiniest spaces of William's little house and particularly his bedroom where he was warm in his cocoon, still deeply sound asleep. It was ten minutes after six when he finally awoke because he had managed to leave his left arm outside the blankets; he finally felt the growing pain of numbness from the cold. Half awake he pulled it back beneath the warm blankets and tried to go back to sleep but it was no use. He was excited because today he thought he would be able to complete his research on Warren's trip. The thought made him even wider awake for he sensed that today would be the day he would make the breakthrough he hoped for.

William arrived ten minutes early at the door of the files department. He was surprised to see that it was ajar with Emmett already sitting behind his desk, a smug look spread across his face.

"You're late detective," he said.

"I... I didn't expect you to be here until eight o'clock."

"Well sometime we do things to make others stand up and take notice. Did I achieve it?"

"You sure did and I appreciate it. I owe you one," he said with a look on his face alternating between guilt and contentment. William smiled as he noticed powdered sugar scattered over much of his desk. "Now, can I trouble you for that last box? It's number nine."

Emmett had already anticipated his request and put the box just out of sight on the floor beside him. "Here you are, sir," he said proudly, as he picked it up and then set it down on the front of his desk with a dull thud. "I hope you'll find what you're looking for in it. By the way, I just noticed from my records that the last person to check this file out was Warren Wheaton himself… and very soon before he died."

William's eyebrows shot up in surprise and a tingle of excitement ran up his spine. "This has to be the one," he thought to himself. He signed for the box and carried it eagerly back to his work area. He was glad no one else was around.

"Let's see now, what does the cover sheet say?" he said to himself as he lifted the cardboard box lid off and looked inside. He was getting more and more excited. It indicated there were only seven cases in the storage box. Cases 145 to 148 involved uniformed and undercover police officers working several drug squads. Warren's name or initials wasn't among them. Case 149 had to do with a robbery/ grand theft case and 150 with a foiled kidnapping. Neither of them had involved Warren either. It was in the log of the last case where his name finally appeared with the hand-written note *"Significance-To-Be-Determined."* It had Warren's initials and the date. He had inserted this material in the box only three days before he was killed in the terrible highway collision.

William began to breathe faster for he sensed that he was really on to something. He lifted the last data folder out of the box and discovered it contained only one item, a light-brown medium-weight manila-colored padded envelope about an inch thick and the size of a small book. Indeed, whatever was inside felt firm like a book. It could only be bent a little, like a thick card-board covered paperback. The envelope itself was sealed shut; for some reason Warren had signed his name across the gummed flap. William was getting even more excited now. Should he open the envelope or let the chief or someone else open it? What if it contained some kind of incriminating evidence against Warren? Was that the reason he had written *"Significance-To-Be-Determined"*? And why had he buried this envelope in this particular file? Did he want to make it harder for someone else to find for some reason?

Then many other questions began to pile up in his mind: "Where did he get it and why did he have this object, whatever it was, in the first place? Was it related to the man he met in central *Weeklun*? Why didn't he tell anyone about it? Why didn't he even tell me, one of his closest friends? I wouldn't have told anyone!" he questioned. "I know he didn't tell Wini or the chief or they wouldn't have asked me to find out about it. It must be a pretty valuable whatever it is."

He felt a little angry at Warren at first for not having trusted him. "Was Warren ever going to tell his secret?" William had no answers at all.

As he thought back about the details of Warren's Round-*Memland* trip he remembered reading about how Warren had hidden in plain sight that brief and ambig-uous phrase in the file folder: *"Significance-To-Be-Determined"*. "Was Warren trying to give a clue about what to look for? Did he write it to himself or to someone else who would come across the file later? Was he still trying to figure out what to do with this thing, whatever it was, when he died?" As before he was coming up with many more questions than answers.

After thinking about them for a long time he decided that he would assume full responsibility and perhaps even protect his partner's reputation. He would open the envelope himself. (Little did he know that by doing so he would violate its provenance as legal evidence. (He didn't yet know that it contained a precious and absolutely unique record of very ancient wisdom about the *Secret of Mem*: the cause, cure for, and aftermath of the amnesia and missing time malady that had plagued the planet from the beginning. It would turn out to be a decision that would change his life forever).

. . .

"Hello. This is Wini Wheaton. Would you please put me through to the chief?"

Hello sir. This is Wini Wheaton. Do you have a minute?"

"Yes of course. It's good hearing from you again Wini. Is everything all right?"

She was excited and spoke quickly. "I'm doing OK, thanks, but the reason I'm calling is that I just found some things of possible importance. One of them was in one of Warren's jackets out in the garage. It could be from his trip years ago and I thought you'd want to know about it."

The chief replied, "Yes, of course, can you tell me what it was?"

"Well, it was a piece of paper all carefully folded up

in a tight wad that he had put in an inside pocket. He must have forgotten about it. I spread it out and read it under bright light... I've got it here with me. I can't make anything out of it but maybe you could."

The Chief thought for a moment and then replied, "Well, I've assigned that case to detective Thomas who you know. Could I have him come by and look at it?"

Wini said, "Sure, that would be fine. Do you know when he might be coming over?"

"I'll have him phone you."

Wini was so excited that she forgot to mention the longer hand written passages she had found in the white envelope hidden in his drawer.

William arrived at Wini's at nine o'clock the next morning, pencil and pad in hand. He only knocked once before she opened the door with a smile and cup of hot coffee for him in her hand. She was wearing a smock and a chef's apron and smelled of cinnamon and almonds.

"Hello William. Come on in and sit down. I've got some breakfast rolls coming out of the oven in a minute or two. They'll go with your coffee."

He took the cup gratefully and followed her into the kitchen. "Man does that smell good," he said. "I can't remember since I've had any fresh-baked goods of any kind." To himself, "I hope she made a lot of them."

She smiled inwardly as she wiped her hands on her apron and looked at the rolls through the glass door of her oven. "They're almost done. Please sit down," motioning toward the small dining table nearby.

"The chief called and said you've found something."

"Yes, I found a sheet of paper last night out in the garage. It was inside a jacket pocket of Warren's and I think it could have come from his trip around *Mem*. The writing on it made no sense to me so I called the chief and he said you'd come over and take a look."

So far William had very little background in forensic investigations regarding safeguarding and documenting the provenance of evidence. So, he didn't know what to do with the single sheet of folded paper she handed him. It now had his and her fingerprints on it. He felt a little self-conscious but he still pulled out a pair of white cotton gloves before doing anything more with it.

"I'm impressed," she said as she watched in fascination." Are those really necessary?"

"I don't know yet. I'm just trying to follow what they taught me in our forensic training class... don't want my own fingerprints on it you see."

"Oh!", She responded with a stricken look, "Shouldn't I have touched it?"

He didn't know what to answer so he made it up and hoped he was right, "Don't worry. You didn't know... so let's take a look at it." He carefully flattened it out on the table top and then read it out loud:

William caught his breath and thought to himself, "This piece of paper came from Warren's daily travel log. Its torn edge matches the missing page there." It was yet another important clue. He knew right away that it continued the message that had been penned on the previous page. "Apparently it was so important that Warren didn't want anyone else to read it," he thought.

about the cause and only sure cure for time and memory loss everyone experiences... everything is presented in a 6" x 9" black leather-bound book that has been entrusted to me... I will hide it until I decide what to do with it.

Then, trying to act as innocent as possible and cover up what he already knew, William said, “Very little of that makes sense to me. I don’t know whether it could be useful to our inquiry. We may need to have it looked at by someone else. Would that be all right with you?”

“Of course. Feel free to take it. I don’t know what to do with it,” she replied.

William had finished off his third cinnamon roll and second cup of coffee before he finally rose and said, “Wini, I really appreciate you called me about this. I’ll let you know if we find out something important, OK?”

“OK,” she replied as she escorted him to her front door and waved good bye. She didn’t show him the other pages from Warren for some reason.

5

The Reverse Side of the Coin

It was fortunate that *Mem's* millions of inhabitants included only a relatively small minority who deliberately disregarded the law. Yet unfortunately, there were some and, as a group, they tended to be more intelligent than the average *Memlandian*, if one could even measure intelligence reliably in a people who experienced long periods of complete memory loss. They also tended to be more pro-active, aggressive and cagy. They operated mostly out of sight behind the scenes while still making lots of money: stealing it one way or another, short-changing others for it, smuggling or counterfeiting it, rigging stock markets, running protection rackets, drugs and girls, or by finding otherwise creative ways to break the law... sometimes just to prove that they could! They were the less noticed reverse side of the coin of *Mem*.

Indeed, these criminals worked hard to stay out of sight except when they couldn't, which wasn't very often. They had learned the hard way that they were in a virtual hot war with the police; from their point of view it was unfair that the police had the law on their side. But, while the criminals had been winning some of the smaller battles, they had gradually been losing the larger war with “law and order.”

They had tried many things.

Years before they attempted to beat the police by hacking into their computer systems. When the police finally found out about it, they not only plugged the holes but, for a time, used the same holes against them. Then they blackmailed a member of Morristown’s police department to spy for them from the inside. They needed to know both strategy and deployment information. But the informant was eventually identified and silently dealt with.

Then the police went on the offensive by planting false information as if it had come from the informant that, fortunately, they had “neutralized.” Their trap failed, however, when the crime bosses met and agreed not to take the bait (it had to do with false details about an armored car delivery of a huge amount of cash to a large bank). More recently, the syndicate used knowledge of the day of the week that each officer experienced memnesia to plan their crime sprees. But, of course *Weeklun’s* police departments had anticipated this and had already assigned members of each team and squad on the basis of non-overlapping days and hours of their amnesia.

The syndicate finally realized that they needed some super overarching advantage over their enemy that would turn the tide, level the playing field, settle the score once and for all, and give them the upper hand. In short, they needed to be able to carry out their many criminal acts without any major hindrance. It wasn’t long before one of their top crime bosses came up with a plan, he thought would achieve all of these objectives.

He lived in a massive villa in southern *Yurland* and was immensely wealthy and powerful because of his virtual control of the country's gambling, prostitution, protection, smuggling, and money-laundering operations. He was born A. G. Manley but quietly changed it to Frank DeBarrock at the age of twenty-one. On a scale of one to ten he had hated the A (for Alphonse) with a score of nine but no scale was high enough for the terribly embarrassing G (for Gushe). He had never forgiven his parents. When he eventually ascended to the top of the criminal chain he went by F. D. or just boss.

Frank DeBarrock was impressive in many ways. Standing just over six-foot one inch this *Yurlandian* was the epitome of a self-made man. His dark-brown hair and eyes, his dark bushy eyebrows gave his craggy face the look of a citified animal looking for some prey. He knew that his appearance frightened most men and he used it to his advantage. He spent at least an hour every day in his own body-building gym.

When he first began working out at a small gym across town Frank was overwhelmed by the array of contraptions that littered the floor, walls, and ceiling. It was like entering a torture chamber of fiends. The stench of sweat and disinfectant almost drove him out on his first visit, but he was sixteen and knew he needed to get buff for what lay ahead. Somehow, he knew he was on the fast track

"Hey kid, you here for some workin' out?" the owner of the gym had called out over the squeaking of the pulleys, labored breathing of the men already straining under great loads, and grunts of others who had "bitten off" far more weight than they could handle trying to show off. His voice had a faintly menacing tone.

"Yeah. What's it gonna' cost?"

Frank never forgot those early years and the long-lasting muscular pains he experienced along with the jibs from the other guys, the few who had had a head start and had persevered. Their taunts had only motivated him to master the hack squat machine that built his adductors, quadriceps, and hamstrings, the hyperextension bench for his quadratus lumborum, multifidi and iliocostalis muscles, the lateral pulldown machine that conditioned his latissimus dorsi and other muscles, and a host of other contraptions that would eventually bulk up most of the other muscles that outlined his growing body. He knew them all by name.

By the age of thirty he saw himself an Adonis, a creature to be both admired and obeyed, marveled at and feared at the same time. That's exactly what he had wanted to happen. That's exactly what he had achieved!

He was overly proud of his physique and one hundred eighty-four pounds of mostly muscle. He detested wimpy men. In fact, they made him angry for some reason. His anger surprised him the first time he recognized it; he couldn't figure out where it came from. But, as the years passed, Frank accepted his anger as a good thing, actually a self-protective response; something to be proud of and used to his advantage.

As he grew in stature and reputation he recognized that without professional coaching his zeal to remain strong would probably dwindle so he hired a full time body builder named Yuri, a giant with muscles even larger than his. Over the years Yuri became his only close confidant and friend as Frank rose in power within the syndicate. The two were inseparable and often seen together at parties and business meetings. Some thought they were business partners others assumed Yuri was his bodyguard. Frank trusted him mostly because he knew that Yuri wasn't as smart as he was. It had nothing to do with trust or honor; Yuri wouldn't know how to outsmart him or blackmail him even if he had wanted to. "Such treachery would never even enter his mind," Frank thought. He took their relationship as a solid fact that he could count on.

Frank's personal gym was a huge brightly lit air-conditioned room on the top floor of his mansion. It had many diffuse-glass skylights but no windows at all. Its door was sound proofed and its walls and floor could be literally mopped down after his daily "torture sessions" that others called exercise. Frank was proud of the fact that he had mastered the extensive language used in body building; he often used it to impress his associates: "cross-crank driven ellipticals with electro-magnetic resistance and maximum control, flywheel driven bikes with hand squeeze-force measurement, kettlebells and treadmills."

Frank rose to power quickly within *Yurland's* large yet invisible syndicate. He used his ruthless power and cougar-like cunning extremely effectively. Unlike his many competitors he also read a lot. In fact, he prided himself on his library of books on every subject that *Mem* could provide. Behind his back his lieutenants nicknamed him "Gefar" (it meant dangerous).

He hired Jerome to serve as his personal, full-time professional librarian; Jerome lived in a special apartment on Frank's twenty-acre compound. His job was to search out virtually every new book that was published on the planet as well as every old book not already in his boss's library (which was already very large) and buy it. Money was no object. Frank could afford every book being printed twice over. He prided himself on his ability to speed read most of them. The rest he assigned to his librarian to read and write an abstract for him. Jerome searched them for certain key words and phrases that his boss specified.

It was because of Frank's excellent memory, perseverance and keen consistent focus on tiny details that he learned about an interesting story that had begun only as a rumor that one of his men had heard recently.

Jerry had just returned from a "business trip" to *Weeklun* over the weekend. "Yes, boss, the job's done.

Everything's goin' to be OK. Oh, and I was talkin' with our guys in Morristown. You know how they've got their ears to the ground."

"All right, so what did you pick up?"

"Well it might not be anything important boss but I found out that someone has been spending a lot more time than usual in certain police files," he replied with barely hidden pride in his low, gravelly voice.

"So what? That doesn't sound important?" It was clear that the boss didn't want to waste time on mere rumors. Yet he also knew that there can be some truth in the smallest of them-the least obvious fact-and that sometimes these truths can add up to something useful. That was the way Frank had gained his power, by putting one and one together and coming up with two and a half! He had always kept the other half whichever way it turned out. He went on, "Get on with it then, Jerry, what else?"

The mobster stood there in his tight-fitting three-piece suit with light brown socks looking frightened and bewildered. He went on, "Well boss, one of our guys was at a local restaurant for lunch. He got to talkin' with another guy who just happened to work in the files division of their police department."

At this both men laughed.

"Just happened?"

"Yeah, that's what he said. After a few drinks the other guy happened to mention that a detective had been coming in lookin' at files related to another detective named Warren Wheaton. Now why would one cop be lookin' for files on another cop whose been dead? That's what I thought was interestin.' That's about it. It's probably nothin' important." He quickly looked down at the expensive rug and his scuffed shoes.

Frank replied, "You may be right but maybe not. It's probably a dead end but I've always liked dead ends.

They're always challenging and I've made a lot of money by going down some of them. I think I'll follow up on that particular lead. Thanks Jerry." He didn't explain to the other man what he planned to do but he knew he had to go to *Weeklun*. He would take Yuri with him; as cover they would nose around several book dealers who specialized in ancient literature. It would make his trip look innocent if anyone should ask. He was only adding to his personal library. And even if nothing turned up, they still would enjoy a dinner in *Weeklun's* most expensive restaurant.

Frank keyed his secretary to come in. Francie was a cute, short blond with eyelashes that wouldn't stop fluttering. She knew very well how to use them.

"Francie, I want you and Jerome to find out everything you can about a Warren Wheaton in *Weeklun*. I was informed that he was in their police department until recently. But don't raise anyone else's eyebrows if you know what I mean." She nodded and flashed her attractive smile first at Jerry, who returned it with his own, and then at him like she always did (it was a part of her job insurance), and then left.

Frank had a hunch that this Warren character might have played some role in getting his brother-in-law arrested and put away several years before. The date and location fit. "I'd love to have been the one who put Warren away," he thought. Jerry must have guessed what his boss was thinking for he snickered and said, "They just got lucky boss."

It was several days later that Frank got the information he had asked for. Francie walked in with a file folder an inch thick and labelled *Warren Wheaton*. She plopped it down on his desk with a thud.

After she left, he sat back in his soft, hand-crafted leather chair and pulled out an expensive cigar. He finally lit it after going through all the preliminary steps one follows to ensure its freshness, moisture content, aroma, and finally, taste. As he watched the first wisps of white smoke curl upward from its glowing tip, he said to himself. "This is going to be an enjoyable morning."

It was over an hour later when he had finally finished absorbing the collection of details about Warren's life that his associates had uncovered. "He led an interesting life, that's for sure. I wonder whether it could all be true?" He read about Warren's cooperation with *Yurland's* Strategic Services Academy in a short newspaper article. His raid had done the syndicate a lot of damage by closing down one of their main seacoast smuggling groups across the border. That clinched it. He was the detective who had closed down his brother-in-law's operation and put him behind bars.

The article also referred to another person involved with Warren but didn't give his name. Frank wondered if finding out might be important.

He thought about these questions so long that a long hot gray ash fell on his leather-covered stationery pad leaving a permanently blackened oval. "That's what I get for concentrating so hard," he thought to himself, but with far more pride than annoyance.

"I wonder whether there's any truth to what the article said about a possible link between *Mem's* amnesia and Warren's around *Mem*-expedition back then. It said they didn't find any differences in time wherever they were; I can't see how there could be any other connection."

At first he simply tossed the possibility off that any part of the story could be true yet he couldn't get the idea out of his mind. There was something strange and fascinating about it. Frank was distracted over the next several days by many other decisions he faced, yet the kernel of that idea wouldn't go away. It grew slowly, creeping back into his mind through all hours of the day and night. And each time it returned he thought about how such knowledge could be used to his advantage. Frank was now hooked.

The two of them made their trip to Morristown but returned only two days later. While Frank and Yuri had enjoyed the meals and the drinks they had struck out. They learned nothing useful about Warren Wheaton or the rest of the story. In fact, the Morristown police had identified Frank's car even as it had first crossed into Weeklun and had followed him during his entire visit. In spite of the tail, which Frank spotted right away, he couldn't stop thinking about getting his hands on the cure for memnesia if there really was one.

6

Blank Pages

Books have been used in many ways. Two of them are to record memories or create new ones. Inked symbols pressed down letter by letter, line by line, page by page-onto all kinds of surfaces-have captured and held memories secure for millennia. Yet whatever form these volumes have taken-plain or ornate, large or small, thick or thin-the books on the planet *Mem* played an even more important role than anyone could have imagined because, between their normal sleep and their spans of memnesia, *Memlandians* had missed much of their life. Somehow it needed to be recorded.

Counting their normal sleep the average *Daytunian* lost consciousness seventy two percent of their whole year while *Weeklunders* lost sixty eight percent. A few *Yurlanders* lost almost one entire year every other year! It was books that recorded what they had missed; they helped to fill in the gaps.

Books also helped to distribute and homogenize knowledge across the culture. This worked to unify them into a more consistent people who shared common morals and ethical boundaries.

Books also had the amazing capability to motivate some of their readers to imagine things that didn't even exist. Imagination was very important on *Mem*. Some science fiction books enticed their readers to try to picture such absurdities as spherical or even odd concave planets. Others led their readers astray into mental mazes that seemed to terminate in insanity or some permanent memory dysfunction. Yes, *Memlandians* loved and needed their books.

Yet there was one unique book, bound in ancient worn black leather and soiled by different caretakers' hands over many scores of centuries that had survived. It revealed the *Secret of Mem*, the only solution for the scourge that held all *Memlandians* captive since the their beginning.

It was really a small tome, measuring only five inches wide by seven high yet it contained the full weight of truth-a truth that could be used to benefit all *Memlandians* or misused to control and make them all slaves.

There was something definitely mysterious about this small and inconspicuous little black book that caused William to realize the importance of what he was about to do. He handled the leather covered tome gently, even delicately. It was sturdy yet ethereal at the same time. He didn't know why he did it but at first he only balanced it on his open left palm... to let it breath. The longer he held it, the more he felt he was holding a sacred object that possessed a power all its own. He wasn't sure that it wasn't radiating some energy to his hand and fingers.

"No, that can't be," he reasoned silently. "It's just an old book. I must be imagining things." (It was eleven thirty on Thursday morning, the day and time he wouldn't be experiencing his own noontime memnesia.)

He didn't know what he might find and was glad he was alone. He put the book down gently on the desk and then slowly opened it. It did nothing-no electrical sparks, no tingling or powerful emanations. It just lay there, an innocent looking thing. Then he carefully began turning its pages; he was awestruck when he discovered that every page was completely blank except for some hand-written notes that lined some of its margins.

His initial thought was that the very character of the strange book was mystical; indeed, its invisible inner heart was complex and beyond belief or at least beyond his understanding.

Later it became obvious to William that the margin comments had been inscribed over many centuries by others who had used ink pens of all kinds armed with strange and exotic nibs that produced beautiful cursive forms, odd-shaped letters, and even foreign words that William didn't understand. "Why do this? Why bind a single book of blank pages together unless the author didn't write anything at all or didn't want his message to be read? Maybe it was supposed to be a diary but then why did those other people only write around the edges of the pages? Why not in the middle of the pages and even fill them up?" William was mystified.

Since its pages were blank William couldn't even be certain about this. "Why write something you didn't want others to read?" he mumbled to himself a second time. "It makes no sense at all."

William wouldn't know until later that there were words printed in it but they were made of a strange substance that became visible only for those who possessed sufficient faith to see them. It was as if the ink had been programmed to keep its secret from those who weren't worthy. Only the hand-written notes in the margins remained visible for anyone to read. It was clear that their authors had none of the creative power that the original source had possessed.

"Mr. Thomas," came the voice of the file clerk thirty feet away. "Can I help you with something?"

William winced at hearing the voice; it had startled him out of his deep concentration. He hadn't realized that his wonder had been so loud.

. . .

He had brought it home to try to make sense of it; he had broken the law. He hadn't signed for it but had hidden it under his coat as he turned the file in and left. He had a vague feeling it was, at least, a valuable historical document; he would require total concentration and quiet. It was seven p.m. and the house was quiet. Granville was splayed across the floor with one eye partly open-watching him. William felt excited again and wondered whether Warren had felt the same when he had opened the book for the first time.

He sat down at his kitchen table, adjusted a nearby table lamp, and slowly and gently turned back the soft leather cover to once again expose its first page. Like all the others it was completely blank! It was on the third blank page that he saw four beautifully penned words:

"*A fiducia gemmas pretiosas*"

They were written carefully in black ink along the inner margin where they would be more protected. William's hands were shaking, his heart beat a rapid drum beat in his ears for he was beginning to realize he was dealing with some kind of very ancient sacred document. The words had been written very long ago in an ancient language; the precise hand that inscribed them must have wanted the words to last through the centuries. It was only his meagre knowledge of languages that gave it any meaning at all: *a precious trust* was his best translation.

"How can I understand it if everything is in a foreign language?" he asked himself. Yet, as he quickly browsed through the following pages, he was relieved to discover that most of the margin comments were written in a much later *Memlandian* language that he understood. There were only a few in strange languages with odd looking symbols or geometric shapes.

"I'd better do this right," he thought to himself. He found a lined tablet and several colored ink pens and markers and returned to the table. "I'll make a list of these comments or whatever they are in their original order." On line one he wrote "*A fiducia gemmas pretiosas*" with (*a precious trust*) inserted beside it in parentheses on his first line.

As he slowly and carefully turned the pages he saw more handwritten notes around the edges of the otherwise blank pages. Some were written so tiny that he had to use a magnifying lens to read them. It was clear that each one showed a different handwriting and presented a slightly different color or consistency of ink. They were fascinating. Many seemed like editors' corrections or perhaps comments to some unprinted line of text nearby.

He was captivated by these comments. The second notation he found was:

"Memlandians have regressed without realizing it. Their pride is the cause."

William wondered what that meant; it would have helped if he knew when it was written and under what circumstances. It sounded to him as if the writer was chastising *Memlandians* while trying to give them a hint about something important at the same time.

Several pages later he read:

"The privilege of being right is a flattery without substance."

Other notations followed:

"Faith is the key that will open the Word."

"Wisdom and truth aren't the product of any single generation."

"Be vigilant because expectations are sometimes contrary to reality."

"Tenyleg meg akarjak tudni oz igazsagot"

As William turned over several more pages he was confronted by bold black symbols that surrounded all four sides of the blank space in the middle. "Man, the writer of that must have been frustrated about something. I'd love to know what he wrote," he mumbled to himself. It would probably take a long time to decipher it. He didn't have the time or the ability so he just copied one line as carefully as he could as an example:

"myj 3d e nv le tius Edoz"

Several pages later he read:

"Credo im Deum"

and deciphered it as best he could as *"Believe in God."* He felt pretty proud of himself and hoped he had gotten it right. "Deum must be Deum everywhere in the universe," he thought.

Still other notations proclaimed:

"Yes! Most people have forgotten their own past."

"Memlandians are prisoners of time."

"Time is a precious trust,
Never take it for granted."

"Why does rage envelope the people?"

"The Secret of Mem is not only truth but time."

"If one doesn't know the truth
one can be lied to many times."

The next to last hand-written comment he found was:

"Hope is the expectation of good results-
Faith is the expectation with best results."

He copied it in his tablet without giving it very much thought.

William went back over the entries and noticed the prevalence of the word "time." He underlined each one. "Did each writer read what the others had written? Maybe they were just copying a common theme or trying to give the word "time" special emphasis for some reason? And how was each person chosen to write in the book in the first place?" he asked himself.

Most of the notes made little sense to him. "They had no meaningful context; they must have been related to some text someplace else," he thought.

William tried to arrange his list of entries in different orders in case there might be some other hidden message. He found none. The more of them he copied the more certain he was that they were written by different *Memlandians* over a very long span of time. But he was mostly puzzled by why they were written where they were on blank pages! He didn't realize that he had become captivated by the margin notes and not the rest of the book. How could he? There was nothing there to see!

He was mentally exhausted and finally closed the book. It was after midnight and he realized that whatever message the book possessed could not be forced out of it. He would let it rest; he would do the same.

7

Up Against the Wall

"Coffee! That's what I need! Coffee is exactly what I need," he said as he headed off to his tiny bachelor kitchen. Fourteen minutes later he returned to the table carrying a cup of hot black instant jolt which he sipped on for a while. As he sat looking at the little book in front of him, he began to let his mind wander. He liked to do that from time to time. It helped him relax. He would open his thoughts to anything that would flow in and then allow it to free-associate with any other thoughts that might also come along. He never interfered with the process because he had always enjoyed what turned up. It was his way of cleansing, no teasing his mind to unwind. He usually felt relaxed afterwards.

For some unknown reason he began thinking about the missing time that everyone had to cope with on the planet. He took another sip of the hot coffee and returned to his free associations. "We've just accepted our missing time and memory as a normal part of life. But should we?" he asked himself. Then he glanced down at his pad and his eyes came to rest on:

"Memlandians have regressed without realizing it. Their pride is the cause."

He was shocked. It was as if, when he asked himself this question, the book had seemed to answer him. "No, that's crazy," he exclaimed as he shook his head. Granville glanced up at him with an earnest look that said, "I'm getting hungry."

"I'll try again to prove it," he said out loud. Once again Granville smiled and wagged his tail. William thought for another moment, hoping that using his free association technique might offer up some new response from the book's margin notes. Then he asked himself the question, "What kind of alibis have I made up in my life to cover my own periods of memnesia?" But instead of trying to answer his own question he quickly looked down at the third entry in his list of notes he had copied from the little book. His eyes immediately fell on:

"The privilege of being right is a flattery without substance.

"What does that mean?" he asked himself. "Well that proves it. There's no connection!" William smiled inwardly as if he had won a bet. He really didn't want to believe a book could talk back.

Nevertheless, there was still a lingering doubt in his mind for some reason. He would try it a third time just to make absolutely sure.

This time he took a larger drink of the now luke-warm coffee, sat back in his chair, closed his eyes (so as to not be biased or tricked by looking at one of the margin notes he had copied ahead of time), and tilted his head way back to relax. He waited. Nothing came to mind. A long, frustrating period of blankness ensued when there should have been a freely flowing association of ideas from his mind or wherever they came from. Finally, the thought slowly entered his mind, "Where should I look to find the answer to Warren's change in personality and his life?" The question surprised him because he didn't believe at all in premonitions or spiritual things and he certainly didn't expect a response from the book that would answer this question. He had tried to be as objective as he could and not "prime the pump" so to speak. It was with some trepidation that he opened his eyes and looked down at his list of margin notes. The first one he saw was:

"The Secret of Mem is not only truth but time."

William was surprised. He had to admit there was a possibility that this margin note might somehow be part of the answer he had asked for. "What were the chances of this happening given all of the other margin notes he had copied from the book? Why did I look at that one in particular?" He knew he must proceed very slowly and not jump to unfounded conclusions. It wouldn't be scientific, yet he was becoming more curious than ever. He realized he was beginning to look at the little book and its margin notes as a kind of OUIJA board. He felt ashamed of himself for harboring such a thought and was glad he was alone.

"So what if the *Secret of Mem* isn't about truth alone but also time?" he asked himself. What does that have to tell me about Warren's personality change? The more he thought about it the more relaxed he got. "There's no relationship between my question and what was written in the book!"

William understood that, like all *Memlandians,* he took his own period of amnesia for granted just as he did his sleep each night. He thought, "Sleep is essential, needed, precious. Yet our short or long periods of memnesia and missing time give us back nothing at all in return, no refreshment like a long deep sleep can give us. It gives us no alertness of mind or quickness of body, nothing at all. It only makes us prisoners of ourselves and of fleeting time itself." And just as he finished thinking this he remembered what the margin note had said: *"The Secret of Mem is not only truth but time."* Once again his heart began to beat faster as he thought about it more. But could the strange force of memnesia be negated or somehow conquered?

8

Eyes of Faith

William had finished copying all of the visible notes from the little black book. He spent several more hours going back over each one. "Could anyone come up with alternative meanings for them that made any sense? Could there be some common thread that connected them or maybe a code of some kind buried within them?" He had noticed that two words seemed to predominate: time and faith.

He hoped that he could find some way to unlock the little book that he had been concentrating on for many hours now. His brain was terribly tired, his eyes sore. He glanced at the clock and discovered it was almost midnight. He had to stop and pick it up again in the morning, but just before he did something strange happened. He felt frustrated and disappointed that he had accomplished almost nothing all day. He thought, "If there's something for me to see here I want to see it!" Just then he happened to glance down at a blank page of the book. Was it his fatigue or something else… but he thought he could barely make out some very faint letters or words on the otherwise blank page?

It was as if they faded into view and then just as quickly disappeared again, just once. He dismissed it as the result of his fatigue.

. . .

Six fifteen seemed to arrive slower than usual for William laid awake most of the night thinking about the strange book and its stranger contents. He had brought it into his bedroom and put it in his top dresser drawer-out of sight beneath a pair of pajamas. He didn't know why he had done that. "Do I really think it's valuable? Am I getting superstitious?" Granville yawned with his familiar sounds, stood up, shook out his long fur for several seconds and whined. William knew what that meant. He needed to go out.

It wasn't until seven a.m. that he finally let Granville back in, retrieved the little book from his dresser and sat down again at the table to continue his search. He had fixed himself a quick breakfast of toast and peanut butter along with half a banana. Now, armed with a fresh cup of hot coffee beside him he felt much more alert than he had the night before. For some reason he didn't understand he had also washed his hands much longer and more thoroughly than ever before.

As he quickly scanned down to the bottom of his list of margin notes he happened to notice:

"Hope is the expectation of good results-
Faith is the expectation with best results."

"What does that mean?" He couldn't think of anything it related to. "It's true that we usually hope we'll get good results, that's just common sense," he said out loud. And there's that word faith again. It must be important somehow. Granville raised his head and smiled in response to his master's voice. "But somehow faith expects best results." He was puzzled by the connections between hope and faith: good and best."

William's closed his eyes tightly to try to see some connection. Nothing came to mind. Then he suddenly remembered last night again.

"Was I hallucinating or did those letters and words on the blank pages really become visible? Of course it isn't possible!" he concluded.

"It was probably because I was so tired yet I'm pretty sure I saw something there just for a second. They were very faint grey words or symbols," he thought to himself. No, it was probably just my imagination. What was I doing just before I saw them?" All he could remember was that he had felt so tired and frustrated that he had literally challenged the book to speak to him. That's when the page began to fill with printed text. It was as if his emotion or his frustrated hope had triggered the appearance. He knew that he had to try it again.

William screwed up his face in mock anger and frustration, took a deep breath and cried, "you blasted empty pages, do something!" Nothing happened. "Maybe it was because I was so tired last night. My emotion just now was about as fake as can be." Then he got another idea. He would try to exercise his faith not his emotion. That was it! He would work hard to expect the best results, just as the writing had said:

"Hope is the expectation of good results-
Faith is the expectation with best results."

Then William reached for his tablet with all of the margin notes he had copied down. There, near the very top he noticed one that he had overlooked before.

"Faith is the key that will open the Word."

Why hadn't he noticed it before? Now, he was surer

than ever that he was on to something. It was faith of some kind, not simply hope or simple belief that was the key. Yet he really didn't know what that special kind of faith was or whether he possessed it.

For William faith was one of those words one heard occasionally but without any need or desire to understand its deeper meaning; one quickly just passes over it. Throughout his youth his parents had almost never used that word in their conversation. They lived a life of hard work and simple unadorned practical beliefs, little else. And so, William had never given faith any serious thought either. Up until right now it had been a rather vague concept only used by a few religious types or perhaps philosophers. But now it had become very important. He wanted to get the little book to speak to him in some way if it was going to. To do this he had to discover what genuine-or at least sufficient-faith was about. (He didn't understand that it is God who provides the special kind of faith that is needed to be able to read the book).

"But how do I do that?" he asked himself. As he sat thinking about it he got an idea. "I'll start with the dictionary. I'll look up its definition and try to have whatever the definition says it is." William laughed at himself as he realized he was trying to work out the meaning of a word he didn't understand by his own behavior. He got out his unabridged dictionary and found:

"Faith: Confidence or trust in a person
or thing; Belief that is not based on proof."

"So, confidence and trust are parts of it along with belief. That's all well and good but it doesn't tell me how to get it." He felt even more frustrated.

At least he could concentrate. He would try to be as

serious and focused as he could to really believe that the book would actually respond to him even though deep down inside himself, he felt such a thing was impossible. His conflicting thoughts made him doubt the outcome. He knew his confidence was wavering. "Nevertheless, isn't being serious and focused kind of a faith response?" he rationalized. Didn't two separate margin notes say much the same thing?" Yet, doubt and skepticism that it would work still lay hidden within the recesses of his subconscious mind. But he would do his best to block out all thoughts of doubt and skepticism that normally rose up so easily within him. He knew he would have to purge a lot of conflicting, distracting thoughts as well. "They can also block my faith," he surmised.

He discovered how hard it was to actually do it.

His years of higher education had planted their invisible seeds of bias and questioning mistrust very deep; they were absolutely against any such irrational belief like the power of faith. "This isn't going to be possible. It's stupid," he thought.

With the book opened and its blank page facing him he looked down and simply closed his eyes for a few moments. As he did so he used the time to relax and hope for something to happen. Then he remembered the words... "*Belief that is not based on proof.*" The words made more sense now. They calmed him. And, as he opened his eyes he noticed words just barely beginning to emerge onto the page. Their appearance was electrifying.

Those who falsely believe they are free are more hopelessly enslaved than those who are willing to reach out for real freedom. Those who know the

Just like last night he couldn't believe it was really happening. And as he focused his troubled mind on what his intellect knew wasn't possible the text faded from view again. He tried it a second time only this time he opened to a new page and rotated the book so that a different angle of light played on its page. He didn't want some stupid illusion to make a fool of him.

Suddenly from nowhere he heard that same voice that he had heard before:

"You can only see it if you
have true faith it is there."

William jumped in fright. His pulse jumped even higher. Now it was a talking book! He was actually listening to a book! "It's crazy. Yet it was the third time that faith was mentioned as the key. Only this time I also heard that it must be true faith, whatever that is."

The voice had shocked and surprised him at the same time. He didn't understand how audible ideas could enter his mind like that. "I'm sure it was audible," he thought. "Am I going mad? Was it an hallucination?" Yet Granville had never moved a muscle or even opened his eyes to look at him when it happened. The whole thing was insane.

He didn't give up.

"I'm going to try hard to really believe that the words are already there on the page," he said out loud quite insulated from how unprofessional and silly he sounded; he was talking back to the voice he had just heard and to the book.

It worked!

it is continually being created and expanding into cosmic space to fill the whole Universe and thereby increase manifold entropy even more? What if it isn't simply another second of time that has already existed since the beginning and then suddenly appears sixty times every minute? What if it's an entirely brand-new, freshly created second made to fill the void that was created by the fleeing, disintegrating jungle animal?

William's pupils dilated, adrenalin flowed into his blood stream, he felt its tingling and was more awake than he had ever been before. It was impossible for him to concentrate on what the text said but only on its existence. Yet, unconsciously he realized that if he could keep it in sight he could eventually understand what it's message was.

As he began to concentrate on each blank page, now he knew he would see something show up… the more he believed this the darker the words became. "I've stumbled onto the key! It has to be my own power of concentration and trust," he told himself. He was very excited. He was working magic.

"I can't believe I've just done it," he said, filled with pride. Even as these words were forming in his mind the printed words on the page dissolved almost instantly back into nothingness.

Once again, he was both elated and frustrated at the same time. Unless he could control himself and his prideful attitude he wouldn't be able to maintain a readable text.

Then the voice spoke again calmly and quietly to confirm this:

"Yes, take your time and control your pride.
Know who it is that lies behind your faith."

William was feeling more and more comfortable listening to the book or to whomever it was; he was not nearly as self-conscious as before. It was a brand-new exhilarating experience.

On one level his rational mind said, "Somehow the

text seems to be made of invisible ink that comes and goes under my control." It gave him a strange and weird feeling of power to make it happen. "Probably no one in all of *Mem's* history has done what I've just done," he said with swelling pride yet again. (Little did he realize that one person in every generation since the book had been prepared had learned to control the book and cause its message about the *Secret of Mem* to become readable).

Something made William look at his list of margin notes again. He had no idea why until he read his second notation again:

> *"Memlandians have regressed without realizing it. Their pride is the cause."*

Suddenly the words made sense. Maybe it was his pride that caused the words to disappear. Pride was acting like a negative force, a filter that worked to block genuine faith. He slowly realized that he had to choose between letting faith or pride predominate if he was ever going to discover what was written in this little book.

As he began to study the main text in earnest now William wasn't as startled as before when he heard the same voice. It seemed to come from everywhere and from nowhere:

> *"You must believe that the wounds of memory lost actually can be healed."*

Then the voice stopped just as abruptly leaving only the tick of the kitchen clock to fill the void-that voice again and then the silence! Nothing more. What did it all mean?

He realized that everyone's period of memnesia and loss of time produced wounds of one kind or another but he had no idea that these wounds could be healed.

It was a brand-new idea to him. Yet, somehow, he believed it.

Then he opened to the first page in the book and, for the first time, was able to read in bold black print what now appeared mysteriously out of the blank paper. It was centered and in darker print:

Beware
"For those who will not learn it will
be a wound that never fully heals."

The message seemed to be related to the message he had just heard. The first one from the voice was positive while the second, printed here, seemed to be a warning. He wondered how one's defiance or stubbornness to not learn something could be like a wound? "It seems to me that the writer was trying to create a boundary to separate mentality from intellect while still treating them both as tangible reality. And what did it mean by learn? Learn what?" (William was about to embark on a life-long journey that would challenge him as nothing ever had before. There was no way he could have known that he could never go back. Like Warren before him, William was being offered answers to the great mystery that lay behind the commonly accepted loss of time and memory everyone on planet *Mem* faced).

And just as had happened before, many other questions flooded into his mind. "Where did this little book come from? Who wrote it and then bound it into a single collection of leaves? Did it have more than one author? What am I supposed to do with it? Maybe I should just put it back and forget it?" Yet he knew he couldn't forget what he had already read and would continue reading to find answers to these and other troubling questions.

William soon discovered that the earlier pages of the

book that were now visible to him presented historical accounts of the very first cases of memnesia; some were written in an unfamiliar language where he had to guess at the meaning of many of the words, other cases described peoples so old they had no nationality, no locality, no clear identity or familiarity to him. Whom-ever wrote the book had taken great pains to record many details; there were places that he had never heard of before, climatic events that had never been described in any of his college text books and when people's names were sounded out they were oddly funny, not at all normal. He thought that somehow the book might have come from a different planet until he suddenly came across the word Compole. It was that one familiar word that caught and fixed his attention firmly to the text. "That word could not have come from another planet," he thought. He knew that Compole was the one spot on *Mem* where the boundary lines of all three nations met; it was their north pole. Today it was a bustling international park with a tall marble obelisk marking the spot. He had been there once with his parents as a kid.

He was fascinated as he read:

> *"Compole preserves part of the mystery of*
> *memnesia. Recover your dearest early love.*
> *Seek its source of power at the proper time."*

The words meant nothing at all to him-like most of the others so far. Yet they whetted his detective's appetite to read further and look for even more clues.

William was lost in time as he continued to read; time had no meaning no significance at all as he read the words that were now visible to him. It was a book that seemed to contain truths from far back in time itself, something like a dam that contains water that sooner or later must flood over and move on. It seemed to be speaking to his own prehistoric memory and the memory of all peoples of *Mem.*

At times he found himself crying unexpectedly. Some of his tears fell on the ancient pages. They were absorbed with those of others before his. He didn't care. He was becoming a new man with a whole new future. The power he found in the little black book was slowly transforming him. Then he abruptly stopped and asked, "Why me? What do I have to offer anyone?" (Warren had asked the same thing without receiving an answer).

As he continued to read much of the text made little sense and it frustrated him. Reading in an early section of the book he found a short treatise on God. He read:

"The possibility exists that God has given Memlandians a conscious spirit and intellect in order for them to try to enter and even control the spatial domain through their imagination or perhaps through virtual or psychedelic control. For God has not only created time, matter, space and energy but He continues to possess and occupy them fully. Each are essential dimensions of His own Being and the product of His infinite creative Being. Even so, time, matter, space and energy, cannot be all that God is. He is still that camouflaged transcendent jungle animal."

"Even if time, space and energy do comprise dimensions of God Himself that does not preclude Him from also existing beyond them. Some may call this His extradimensional Omnipresence and Omnipotence. So, where is God right now? Some call this place 'heaven' which is clearly a spatial word. Others call it 'eternity,' a temporal word. If both of these are true then it's likely that without God there can be

neither time nor space. Can there be a Creation without a Creator? Can there be existence without time? Without it I cannot even exist to write these words to you? You will find there is something extremely mysterious about the matters in this book."

William was both fascinated and confused by these novel ideas. "What is the camouflaged transcendent jungle animal all about?" he asked himself. "And why would the writer spend any effort writing about God and His presence in space or matter, time or energy?"

The farther he read the more confused he became. William was so perplexed that on an impulse he turned back to pages near the very end of the book to see if they were any easier to understand. He was shocked to see that several of them were filled with columns of numbers and letters in tiny hand-written script and nothing else:

rs44756911	1	846808	T	C
rs13303369	1	852875	T	C
rs4970461	1	852964	G	G
rs7537756	1	854250	A	G
rs7418179	1	858801	A	G
rs1110052	1	873558	T	T
rs7523549	1	879317	C	C
rs2272756	1	882033	G	G
rs61769752	1	883091	G	G
rs76456117	1	887059	G	G
rs3748595	1	887560	C	C
rs3748597	1	888659	C	C
rs13302957	1	891021	A	A
rs267598748	1	891344	G	G
rs13303106	1	891945	G	G
rs4970371	1	893280	A	A
rs13303010	1	894573	A	A
rs6696281	1	903104	C	C
rs28690976	1	903245	A	G
rs6696609	1	903426	C	C
rs28391282	1	904165	G	G
rs267598759	1	906168	G	G
rs28504611	1	908414	C	C
rs28687780	1	908823	G	G

rs28477686	1	910394	T	C
rs56028034	1	916662	A	C
rs11575897	24	2655180	G	G
rs104894976	24	2655248	G	G
rs104894973	24	2655265	T	T
rs104894966	24	2655308	C	C
rs104894956	24	2655319	A	A
rs104894967	24	2655325	C	C
rs104894964	24	2655328	T	T
rs104894972	24	2655361	C	C
rs104894974	24	2655362	C	C
rs104894958	24	2655368	G	G
rs104894970	24	2655371	T	T
rs104894959	24	2655375	G	G
rs104894965	24	2655436	C	C
rs104894968	24	2655442	A	A
rs104894969	24	2655453	C	C
rs104894957	24	2655467	C	C
rs104894971	24	2655592	C	C
rs104894975	24	2655633	A	A
rs104894977	24	2655641	G	G
rs2534636	24	2657176	C	C
rs569336697	24	2657349	T	T
rs1800865	24	2658271	G	G
rs867128490	24	2658285	C	C
rs35840667	24	2661306	T	T
rs2253109	24	2661694	G	G
rs796363895	24	2661836	C	C
rs35067692	24	2663685	T	T
rs759582844	24	2668224	A	A
rs2058276	24	2668456	T	T
rs746714434	24	2669716	C	C
rs13303871	24	2679100	G	G
rs776391000	24	2696497	C	C
rs747730726	24	2697625	G	G

"What do they mean?" he asked himself as he shook his head in bewilderment. Then he noticed three margin notes written on the same pages as the table of numbers. "Maybe they were associated somehow with the tables because of their nearness," he reasoned. They said:

"This truly was a kind and loving person"

"A Le Luel-a, A Le Luel-b"
"Seek new science for your answer"

While they must have made sense to the ancients they meant nothing at all to William. "This book makes it awfully clear that we've really regressed in our knowledge. I hope these numbers aren't important," he mumbled as he turned back to earlier pages again in frustration.

He realized that his journey through this book wasn't going to be as easy as he first thought. He wasn't a linguist at all or even much of a scholar and he knew he couldn't take the book to others who might be able to decipher them. It was his sacred trust alone.

Even though William had no great intellect he did notice several things from reading this wondrous little book. First, it was clearly authentic-an ancient book written by primitives on *Mem.* Yet, the writing was spiritually advanced in practical wisdom and truth. He perceived that today's *Memlandians* actually had regressed in many ways without realizing it. In their pride they had either forgotten or voluntarily let go of their earlier spiritual roots.

He also noticed that it was a very mysterious book-interwoven with arcane words that had lost much of their meaning over the eons. They were hard to understand without the benefit of knowing the earlier culture in which it was written. It was as if modern day *Memlandians* had eschewed their own past even as they marched forward.

He had discovered yet another truth- its contributors spanned many centuries each adding some practical truth without contradicting any previous teachings or advice. "Wisdom and truth are not the product or possession of any single generation," he had reasoned.

He was gaining wisdom himself as he realized that everyone has a need to believe in something. The wisdom that underlies principles for living that he found in this book not only reached out toward but seemed to join the religious with the secular; simple faith and acceptance of an unseen but loving Creator God could fill the absolute emptiness of unbelief that has no hope at all.

And finally, William discovered that the ancient wisdom recorded in this book was still valid. The passage of time and constant changes in culture hadn't erased or changed these truths. Time hadn't changed them-only the people had changed.

The hours flew buy unnoticed, pulling the yellow shafts of sunlight from the floor beneath his feet to the wall and slowly upwards and then, gone altogether. He didn't notice. He was captured by the precious object lying before him. His mind was trying to grasp both the ideas that were expressed clearly as well as its cryptic phrases that made little sense, its words and symbols written in an ancient language along with its handwritten margin notes.

It was in the early hours of the next morning that he suddenly looked at his watch; the position of its hands forced him to accept his utter fatigue. "I can't do this any longer," he mumbled. His bloodshot eyes hurt and his neck that had been bent forward for so long finally called out for relief. He massaged it for several minutes while stretching for renewed circulation. As he did so the text faded from sight again.

Even though he was exhausted he felt alive and tingling all over. It was like getting sprayed with a mist of tiny particles of mild acid or alcohol. It was a totally exhilarating new experience.

He stood, picked up the little book gently and replaced it in its original envelope marked "*Miscellaneous –Closed Cases*" in which Warren had so carefully hidden it. He put Granville out one last time and put the book in the middle drawer of his dresser underneath several dress shirts. "Hey Granville, come here boy," he called out. Seconds later his faithful companion padded in looking up into his bloodshot eyes with a friendly grin showing clearly on his shaggy face. William said, "You are going to be my guard dog tonight, you understand?" Granville wagged his tail.

Then William locked up the house, turned out the lights, closed his bedroom door and pulled a chair over and wedged it beneath the knob. Then he placed a small woven oval rug for Granville to sleep on in front of the door as well. The furry four-legged guard came over and laid down on it obediently. To get in someone would have to push the chair and Granville out of the way and by then he would be awake. William felt safer already. His last act before lying down to sleep was to get his service pistol out of his holster that was hanging from a hook in his closet and place it on the night stand beside the bed. Then he laid down to try to sleep.

He had never felt insecure in his small house before. In all the years he had lived there he had never had any reason to be afraid but something had changed. Now he was the sole possessor of that little book containing its priceless treasures from the distant past and its timeless truths that could change the entire planet.

9

The Reverse Side Revisited

The cellar smelled of stale cigar smoke, mildew and damp rotting wood and its ceiling beams were pitted and half-bored through with ancient worm holes. Each beam was covered in gray-white spider webs spun over many decades. Their silver strands seemed to bind the beams together with complex geometric patterns but without any strength; the parallel beams seemed to sag ominously under the weight of the two stories above. The one bare light bulb hanging from the center of the ceiling spilled weak yellow illumination over the rough boards of the floor to make the gaps between them even more obvious and bare. The room had no windows and only one door (it had been built to serve as a secure storage room for cases of liquor. The floor above was a bar). The only furniture consisted of a small table and two spindly chairs. The meeting was to take place here.

Three men had arrived at the back door of the building almost at the same time through the dark smelly alley. They arrived from opposite directions.

One was over six feet tall with a square clean-shaved face, muscular build beneath his expensive dark gray suit and white spats that crowned his polished wingtip black and white shoes. The second man was shorter and heavier, his frame solid and square. He had shaved that morning yet his blue stubble had already reappeared to give him an even more ominous look under the dim yellow light of the single bulb above the door. He wore a medium brown suit and tie with a darker brown vest. He didn't seem to care that his shoulder holster and gun bulged visibly. The third man was a gigantic hulk who remained quietly in the shadows.

"Well, you're on time," Frank said with a sneer that the other man couldn't see in the dim light.

"Yeah, you said nine didn't cha?" replied the shorter man.

"Let's get inside. It's cold out here... Yuri, you stay here and watch," Frank said as he led the other man through the side entrance and into the low-class bar. A NO ADMITTANCE sign hung at an angle by one nail over the door. The hinges squeaked loudly and then the heavy steel door slammed shut behind them. They descended the stairs to the basement as silently as they could but the shorter man's limp still shook the stair's floor boards. They walked down a short narrow hallway toward an unmarked door.

"After you my friend," said Frank with a very slight bow as if to gain the upper hand that is marked as courtesy in more gentile societies. Then he reached in and found the ceiling's light switch and shut the door behind them. He had been there once before. He used his handkerchief to wipe the dust off one of the chairs and sat down at the spindly table. He motioned for the other man to do the same. He said, "Curtis, I appreciate your coming tonight. I don't want to waste a lot of your time or mine with preliminaries so let me get to the point why I called the meeting."

"Yeah?" he replied nodding his head and sizing Frank up. They had only met once before but knew each other's reputation, neither were good. Curt knew that Frank was among the top bosses in *Yurland* and as fearless and brash as he was smooth and friendly when he needed to be. "So, what's up F.D.?" he asked.

Frank waited for a long time before he responded. He had learned long before how to gain a moral advantage. He was in control of time which allowed him to size the other person up while putting him on the defensive. He offered Curtis a cigar. He declined. So, Frank lit one up for himself. He enjoyed going through his usual sacred ritual while showing off his expensive cigars. Then at length he exhaled a long stream of fragrant smoke and finally answered. "Well Curtis, I've got a job for someone who doesn't have any record, who is from *Weeklun* and doesn't officially know me, and who has some special skills, like the kind you have. I'm impressed with your many ways to avoid arrest. And the job pays very well too."

Curt's eyes lit up by the complement but even more by the word pay. He was getting more curious but tried not to let it show. "It's never a good idea to sign-on too quickly. One never knows what the unexplained side of any job might be," he thought to himself. He smiled only slightly.

Frank studied the other man through two more long puffs on his cigar before going on. He loved to let the smoke out in long slow smooth breaths that made the vaporous cloud hang in the air awhile. Across from him he saw a middle-aged man with a broken nose that had never healed; dark brown eyes and bushy eyebrows that spanned above his nose gave him a fierce primitive look; long dark brown hair that was combed back and tied in a short pony tail. Frank thought to himself, "He'd be immediately identified by any witness without a doubt except for the fact that he was wearing a wig, false eyebrows, dyed hair, and had faked a false limp." Frank knew his reputation and his skills and they fit perfectly for what he needed done.

"And so what do you need doin?"

"I'm only going to give you enough background information now so that you'll see how important what I want is," he began. "There's was this police detective here in Morristown who discovered a little book or manuscript or something like that some years ago. His name was Warren Wheaton. I don't know very much about him yet except a rumor. It was that after he returned from a special long-distance trip he was said to have found something that had changed his whole personality. He became a totally different man."

Curt gave him a strange look as if to say, "So what? Get to the point."

"Well, some years later he was killed in a head-on collision one night. I can only tell you this, that it was deliberate, a hit-job set-up by someone I won't identify. They thought he had this book or whatever it was with him. But they didn't figure on both drivers dying. Someone wanted that little book pretty badly but it had disappeared. Now I want it. It's that simple." Frank said.

Curt replied, "How can any book be that important?"

"That's none of your business. Your job is to find it and get it for me. That's all."

Curt cocked his shaggy decoy-haired head to one side and squinted at Frank; after a long pause he said, "And how am I supposed to find that book or whatever it is unless you tell me a lot more than that. I've got to have more to go on."

"You'll find everything I know here in this package," he replied as he handed a manilla envelope across to him. "Read it. It should be enough. After that you can ask more questions if you need to, but from now on you can't contact me. You can reach my associate through this number," he said with a frown as he handed Curt a slip of paper with a phone number and key to use for its encryption. "You do know how to do an encrypted call?"

His question brought an instant response in Curt's stiffened body language. He had been insulted, treated like an amateur. He didn't reply at first but only pursed his lips. He didn't like Frank at first and his question and whole demeaning attitude hadn't changed his opinion. At length he finally muttered, "Yes, of course."

"Good. Here's a retainer that should get you through the next several weeks," Frank said. He handed him another thick envelope.

Curt opened it and flipped through the stack of newly printed hundreds in *Mem's* international currency. When he was satisfied, he nodded, put the envelope in his inside breast pocket and said, "I'll be in touch."

Neither man liked the other; they didn't shake hands. Frank simply said, "That's it. I'll look forward to hearing from you as soon as possible."

Then they both left the building into the dark alley where Yuri, Frank's associate, was still waiting.

. . .

When he got back to his hotel room Curt opened the large envelope and dumped its contents out on his bed. They included a photocopy of an official Morristown Police Department file entitled *Close-out Summary - Official Round-Memland Expedition,* (its cover had been stamped 'LIMITED DISTRIBUTION' in large red letters), a list of names, addresses, phone numbers, and computer addresses (several were marked with an asterisk), and a single sheet that briefly described what he was supposed to locate and steal. It was a notebook or some kind of bound volume supposedly with information about the memory of *Memlandians*. That was all he had to go on!

Curt knew that it wasn't enough no matter how good a thief he thought he was. If Frank didn't know more than this it would be a waste of time to take the job. He had to find out more if he could before he backed out so he dialed the number on the slip of paper and then punched in a long string of numbers that would make his call impossible for others to understand. He heard a strange buzzing sound at the other end and finally a click.

"Yes? Who is this?"

"Curt... the *Mem* job," he replied, wondering whether the encryption really worked. "Maybe I should have used my voice synthesizer after all," he thought.

The male voice at the other end was deep and resonant with a slight foreign accent, "probably a *Daytunian,"* he thought. He said, "OK, go ahead, what do you want?"

Curt answered, "Who am I talking to?"

"I am Yuri. I am an associate. That's all you need to know."

"Well, Yuri I went through the material the boss gave me and there isn't enough information to go on. That's why I'm calling."

Yuri replied, "You'll need to talk to someone else about that. I can get him at this number when you'll call back at seven p.m. tonight. His name is Jerry. Good bye." And he hung up abruptly in Curt's face.

Curt wasn't used to being treated like that and it quickly elevated his anger to the boiling point." They should call me back," he thought. "But I need this work right now so I'll have to go ahead as long as they can give me enough information.

It was seven p.m. when Curt obediently phoned the number he had been given and asked for Jerry. After another long pause... "Yes, with whom am I speaking?" finally came the reply from the other end. The voice was male, polite and with a tinge of soft femininity.

"You're talking to the guy your boss told you about. I'm not giving my name over the phone no matter how secure you think this line is." Curt was still simmering inside; he didn't mind letting it show.

"I'm sorry sir but the boss, as you call him, never informed me about anyone working for him. Can you perhaps tell me what the subject might be?"

Curt was getting even madder. He almost screamed into the phone, "The subject you idiot? The job was to locate a particular book about some *Mem* expedition or something! Yuri told me to call back tonight."

"Oh yes, now I understand. I'm very sorry indeed, sir. Please do forgive me. Yuri did mention your call at seven and that you had a question that I might be able to answer. You see, I helped retrieve the *Close-out Summary* of the police report that you have," he admitted with some pride.

Curt calmed down a little and thought, "What a way to run a business! F.D. can't be that muddle-headed." Out loud he finally said, "Well Jerry, in order for me to satisfy your boss I need more information than he gave me. Are you sure this is a secure line?"

"Oh yes sir, we have it verified several times a week. There's no need at all to worry about that," Jerry replied with full assurance in his smooth gentle voice.

Curt still wasn't sure. "All right then, I need you to tell me everything you know about a small book or magazine or something that a Warren Wheaton of the Morristown Police Department is said to have found a long time ago, I think it was during a hike around *Mem*. That's all I know so far but it isn't enough for me to do my part of the job."

Jerry replied, "I see. Well... I've been working on that same event for him and here's what I've found out.... "

Curt hung up after another five minutes; he had learned very little new or useful information except for one... the name of Warren's police partner. It was William Thomas. It was weak but at least it was something he could get started on. It might lead to other leads.

Curt got to work right away although he had doubts that Warren's partner would be much help. He read the other documents Frank had given him over again and couldn't find any mention of a William or Bill Thomas. He must have joined the force after that expedition around *Mem*. "I wonder what that official expedition was really about?" he asked himself. "Maybe there is a link with the book there."

. . .

Two days later he had located William's little two-bedroom house and sat in his car across the street from it. He used a false ID (he always carried it with him) to rent a non-descript, two-door sedan with deeply tinted windows. He waited hour after hour to catch a glimpse of the him. "So what if he is a detective," he thought, "that's never been a problem for me before (Frank had carefully selected him for this job because he had never been arrested and was a master of disguises. He could go into a phone booth as a short stocky street bum and come out a tall, well-dressed banker.) "I'll case his place to check his routine, office hours and whoever he may be living with."

After several days of almost constant surveillance Curt knew what time his dog went out to do his business, what William's favorite shirt color was, what he drove, how he drove (he followed him twice), where he parked, who he waved at, where he shopped and even what kinds of food he liked (once he even followed him around the shopping aisles), and most importantly what his day and time of memnesia was. He had managed to collect a long list of facts. From this distance William didn't look like any threat at all.

"I think I need to wrap this up and look for other leads," he thought to himself. "I'll give it a couple more days just to be sure I haven't overlooked anything.

10

The Secret of Mem

"Well Chief, I'm still looking into things that we talked about and I'd like one more day if that's all right, and I'll be working from home," he said.

"Have you made any progress yet?"

"Well, yes and no. I don't want to talk about it over the phone but I'll fill you in when I come in. I can be reached on my cell anytime."

"Yes, do that."

They hung up. It was Wednesday.

William stayed home the next day so he wouldn't be distracted. He was so preoccupied by the wondrous tome that his appetite dwindled to virtually nothing; he lived mostly on black coffee. He was also less and less distracted by noises in the street outside.

Even though the book had given him a growing awareness that memnesia might be conquered William still wasn't absolutely convinced. Although he was now able to read the words of the book that were made possible by his immature (yet growing) faith-or perhaps from his firm conviction that the words actually existed in the first place-he sensed that he still didn't possess the level or quality of faith that would make it possible to actually overcome memnesia. He was coming to recognize that to do that called for a different kind of faith. He didn't know if he had that kind.

"How could the ancient or ancients who composed these words have developed such a superstitious and legendary explanation for memnesia? They had to be wrong!" his rational mind reasoned. "Modern science knows better. Memnesia has to have some biochemical or neurological etiology," he concluded. And as these thoughts came to him he marveled as he saw the words on the page in front of him melt away again.

Like everyone else on *Mem* William had willingly accepted the belief that science was the final arbiter for things like this, scientific findings had to be right. The myths and legends of the past couldn't possibly be true or as accurate.

But at the same time something inside him prompted the thought, "But, what if today's scientists are wrong? What if ancients knew about things that today's scientists hadn't yet discovered? What if there really is another set of rules that also govern reality? What if the Creator God of *Mem* had come closer to them than to us today?" As hard as he tried, he wasn't able to get these questions out of his mind.

Just like many other *Memlandians* William wavered in his infant faith. At times he felt he needed the security of what was familiar; it was a need that came from his cultural upbringing, schooling, peer pressure, and limited imagination. Memnesia had become a hidden perpetual self-confirming personal bias that was accepted by everyone as unchangeable unavoidable, a kind of psychic inertia. Yet, the little black book was beginning to open his eyes to the possibility that this wasn't true.

William had read about research that had shown that brain tissue actually shrinks in a progressive disease known as Memstenitis (Alzheimer's Disease). The ventricles get larger while the cells of the hippocampus degenerate along with memory, language ability, judgment, bodily functions and behavior. Proteins that become misfolded cannot cross the blood-brain barrier. He knew that the whole process in *Memlandians* usually took from eight to ten years before death imposed its final demand. And yet the little book didn't mention any of this. How could it? There was no science or microscopes or genetics or biochemistry yet. The book did seem to be saying that memory didn't reside in brain tissue alone but also within an ethereal spirit that inhabited every cell of the body along with its many fluids. In fact, intracellular fluids were said to play an exceptional role. And, according to the book, memory in every *Memlandian* was also a special gift from God, given to each individual sometime before birth, exercised through all of life and then returned to Him at death for safekeeping.

He was amazed by the spirituality that seemed woven through its lines. It boldly proclaimed the reality and solidity of the Spirit of God as if the author had seen and felt it. Its spirituality was presented without apology or excuse but only as simple truth. William knew that these kinds of ideas conflicted with current science. He himself still felt conflicted, confused.

He read about the many ways *Memlandians* had tried to find their own cures for their loss of memory and time over the centuries and how they had eventually given up. "Did our progress go into reverse or just stop? I really doubt that people are that different today," he reasoned. But the more he contemplated what the book said the more he found himself taking its side.

He slowly began to see that the negative biases skepticism and doubts people have toward any new teaching of truth could end up shackling them forever. Their blindness and indifference could insulate them from the change that they so desperately needed, change that could come from within this book and, ultimately, from within their own illuminated hearts. He asked himself, "How could these truths have been rejected or at least overlooked for so long?" (There's no way he could have known that Warren had asked himself the same question years before).

William recognized that most *Memlandians* had long since forgotten their spiritual past. The more he read the more convinced he became that it was their deliberate ignorance or denial of God's own Spirit within them that had contributed to their cognitive malady. He found this truth stated clearly on page seventy-three in the book:

"Let God's Spirit become yours
and then never forget."

He was beginning to feel a little anxious about and even annoyed with these short pithy sayings that punctuated the text from time to time. But he had to admit that they hit pretty close to home. "A lot of them seem like they're aimed right at me." He was surprised at his own irrational reaction to this and began to feel like the truths of this innocent looking little book were taking him captive; he didn't like it at first even though he wasn't sure what many of them really meant.

He continued to absorb the truths of the little black book slowly and in little bites. Short refreshing breaths of it were all he could handle without becoming intoxicated, overcome with a mixture of confusion and a new kind of overflowing joy. He could tell he was changing. Something was slowly happening deep down inside himself. He didn't know what it was but it was wonderful. It uplifted him, freed him as if a weight was being lifted off his shoulders; the more he read the lighter and freer he felt. He was slowly becoming a brand-new person.

Each time he opened the blank pages to read the faster its words emerged into clear view. It was reinforcing his new found faith and belief in a way that he couldn't take any credit for himself. It was as if the book was encouraging him to have faith in it. "I'll bet it's God Himself who is the source of my real faith," he thought.

(William didn't know it yet but the sacred trust to keep the little black book secure and to administer its truths for another generation had just been transferred to him. It happened because his thought had been pure and innocently offered without pride or self-focus. From now on he would face the same challenges and stresses that Warren and so many others before him had faced. He had emerged from his own shell and was becoming the man God had called him to be instead of the quiet introverted passive academic book worm computer nerd of the past.)

One powerful thought kept returning to his mind: "Memnesia and missing time don't necessarily have to be an inevitable affliction." It seemed to be one of the central truths in the book. It opened a brand-new perspective to him, a new way of looking at his own loss of time and memory as well as everyone else's. Their periods of "unconsciousness," "obliteration," and "mindlessness," had become so embedded in everyone's psyche that these symptoms were not simply tolerated but had become expected, taken for granted and even looked forward to by some.

William was intrigued when he read that the principles the book offered to cure memnesia had been disclosed publicly only once, countless eons before. It took place at Compole. He discovered this fact not only within the following text but also in a brief margin note nearby that anyone who opened the little book could easily read whether or not they possessed the needed faith. This text read:

"The message offered here was shared with the all inhabitants of Mem very soon before the Compul tree was destroyed by lightning and fire. The growing number of Mem's tribes gathered and listened patiently and then rejected its message as foolishness. That is when they all forgot. The time was not yet ready for them. Another time may come when people will be more open minded and less prideful. Until then this book must be closed to all except its faithful keepers."

On the next page he almost missed seeing a very small, faintly-inked note that had been written in the margin beside this historical fact:

"I am proud to be the keeper
for the first generation."

It was the only margin note William found using the first personal pronoun! It must have been the brave soul who had tried to share the book's truth at Compole with the peoples of *Mem* so long ago. "I wonder whether he lived out his life or was eventually killed by them in their frustration and rage?"

Someone else had written another margin note nearby that proclaimed:

"If one doesn't know the truth one
can be lied to many times."

William knew that an unbelieving culture can lie to itself in many ways. He smiled inwardly as he thought about it. "Man, that really is true. It looks like my ancestors have been lied to a lot since then." He pondered these words for a long time; they raised many more new questions. "I wonder if it was because of simple ignorance, willful opposition by some individual or group, an inept presentation of these truths to the masses or some other reason that my ancestors rejected the freeing message this book offered to them?"

He wasn't surprised to discover, both from several margin notes and the printed text nearby that none of the later custodians of the book had ever again tried to bring this wondrous message to all the people. He found the reason why on the following page where it described how most of them had been persecuted as heretics who opposed the long-standing and firmly established customs of the people. "I guess, sometimes clinging to truth can be dangerous," he thought. In short, the people of *Mem* preferred what was normal and familiar to what was new and frightening to them because it called for faith they didn't have. They didn't want to change.

William now realized that he, too, had been offered the privilege of becoming the next keeper of the *Secret of Mem.* His decision was calling him to step forward into a new future armed only with his hope for the expectation of good results and enough faith to expect the best results. "That's what true faith is really comprised of. That's what brings this text truly alive." He had finally put it all together and answered his own question.

At first William had almost no faith because of his upbringing, schooling, culture, peer pressures, his natural tendency toward skepticism and limited imagination. Yet, it was what he learned from the little book that had planted the seed of a new and deeper faith in his heart.

As William's faith continued to grow in breadth and depth the text became even darker and clearer than ever. It seemed to be sending him a visible reinforcement to encourage his expanding faith. William surprised himself for he found out that he really did possess a simple uncomplicated faith but hadn't realized it. It alone and not his intense concentration intellect pride or will-power was seeking the power of God to overcome his own memnesia. The little book only helped to point out the pathway to him.

He slowly began to notice an even larger and more exciting message emerging from the text. "This is the power to change the lives of others as well as myself," he had concluded. It was a discovery more exciting than anything he could have imagined. He was beginning to realize that he had discovered the cure for everyone's memnesia and it was centered on personal faith and trust in God and His truths. He thought, "Right here, in the middle part of the book, are instructions on how to help others abolish their memnesia and replace it with its cognitive and emotional opposites: A clear and beautifully deep vision of reality along with joy and peace, security, productivity (because time itself had been returned to them), and most of all, memory because they would be fully conscious and could retain what was going on around them. The millions and millions of hours of consciousness that would be reclaimed would revitalize every aspect of life on *Mem.*"

As William continued thinking about what he read he wondered whether Warren had felt the same way he was feeling right now. "Did he realize the importance of these messages? Had he been able to translate and make sense out of the handwritten notations that populated the margins of the pages? If he had maybe that was the reason he had become so positive and hopeful. Yet why hadn't he shared the contents of the book with anyone else?"

William was feeling more and more excited as he thought about what he would do if he finally did succeed in mastering the cure himself. "I'm going to be the first to try it out," he thought out loud, "Whether or not I ever tell anyone else I've got to be sure it really works!"

William read on through the little book slowly and carefully taking notes along the way. He remembered having read earlier about specific instructions on how to be cured of memnesia. But the first time he read those passages they didn't make much sense and he glossed over them. All he saw then were rather vague references that pointed him toward self-control, kindness, patience, selflessness, love and even prayer. But now, after more meditation about these personal traits, he realized he had been trying too hard, looking much too deeply for the answer. "What if the special kind of simple faith that I've discovered, that makes the pages appear, is the only key that is needed? If this is true, I guess that this means memnesia is the result of not having faith," he reasoned.

The more he read the more amazed he became at the basic simplicity behind the secret of memnesia as well as how all *Memlandians* had been blinded by this simplicity. Perhaps its simplicity had made the truth invisible to them. "But I don't know if being able to read these blank pages because now I'm sure I can is the same as believing I can cure my own memnesia! The two may not be the same thing." He would try to find out, but in the privacy of his own home.

As he read farther into the fascinating text, he continued to feel a warmth inside. (He didn't know it yet but it was the warmth that comes from knowing God as a friend).

William recognized that accepting the *Secret of Mem* was something like trying to see two things at different distances in sharp focus at the same time. He knew that people's eyes weren't capable of doing that. Apparently, neither were the brains of the people of *Mem*. They had simply given up on accepting any change for the better in exchange for satisfying their immediate need for normalcy.

It was several hours later that his eyes fell on the next to last paragraph in the book. It began:

> *"Their hearts and their stomachs were full and they forgot me. If only they had continued to do the works they had done at the beginning."*

"What in the world is that about?" he murmured out loud, perplexed. Then he noticed two small, almost inconspicuous, letters written in black ink near the lower edge of the last page in the book. They were:

W. W.

He could only guess whose initials they were. In equally small letters near-by was written:

"My self-control method."

"I think I'll give up for tonight. It was after midnight yet again.

11

The Mistake

Everyone makes mistakes. Apparently, it's an integral part of life throughout the entire Universe. One occurred on the planet *Mem* that was particularly tragic, a slip that could have cost William his life and the great secret he had been carrying.

. . .

Saturday dawned sunny and bright. William awoke only because Granville had padded over to the side of his bed and nuzzled his hip incessantly and then whined a particularly loud whine. It was clear he needed to go out-side badly. "All right, my friend," he said groggily as he slowly slid out of bed with stiffness and effort and into his slippers. The floor was extremely cold. The two headed for the front door together. He knew his four-legged friend well. He would be back scratching at the door soon and then leading his master into the kitchen for his snack.

After William had showered and shaved and let Granville back in for his ritualistic morning snack, he put the coffee pot on and ate a bowl of cereal. He still wasn't fully awake by the time he had finished his first cup. Finally, he returned from his bedroom carrying the little black book and looking forward to finding the section he had marked the night before. Its title was: *"Cure: Steps to Overcome Memnesia."* He had read the pages over several times last night but wanted to read them again.

William opened to his first marker. The page was completely white and without any margin notes. "I know I believe in the power of this miracle," he began in a quiet calm, almost prayer-like voice. He was serious and had almost no doubt that his faith was sufficient. He paused again as he held his head over the blank page; his eyes were closed as he relaxed and concentrated just as he had before. He thought to himself, "If You want me to see the truth please give me the faith I need." His prayer for faith, by faith, for that is what it was, effected the miracle; the text came into view slowly but surely! And without thinking or planning to do so he said, "Thank you, God." He surprised himself. It was the first time in his life that he had actually talked to God. His heart was racing just as it had the other times that the printed text came into view.

He had noticed previously that the little book was divided into three sections: Causes, Cure, Cautions. Some of them were interspersed with comments such as warnings, advice about misusing the teachings and exhortations regarding the future introduction of its principles to the general public. He read several of the cautions with particular attention:

> *"Very great care must be taken to prevent these principles from falling into the hands of anyone who would abuse them for personal*

gain. You must use your new gifts of faith and discernment to assess the true motivations of others who desire to know them."

"When in doubt always err on the side of concealment and withdrawl of these teachings."

William appreciated writings like these for they were unmistakably clear. He continued to read slowly and carefully. He knew that today was Saturday again, his day of experiencing memnesia around noontime, and that he would be locked within his trance for around ten minutes. This was his chance to see if the instructtions really worked.

As both hands of the clock approached twelve he started to follow the steps of the Cure. Even as he did so he began to feel different. There was a slight dizziness at first. His head began to swim and his vision blurred slightly, yet it wasn't at all unpleasant nor was it familiar. The longer he read he found that his head actually became clearer, his hearing and vision sharper. He felt more alert than he ever had before, even after three cups of really strong morning coffee... but this time there was no associated buzz. By the time noon arrived William was wide awake. He wasn't unconscious! He was ecstatic! "Hey Granville, let's go out for a walk!" he called out. Granville wagged his tail, got up, and went to the front door to wait.

"I really need to make sure," he said to himself. "To think that I've never spent a Saturday noon awake. What will it be like? Anyway, the fresh air should do us both some good. If I can come back in five or ten minutes and remember everything I saw it will prove that it really works."

Both were excited as they left the house. Granville ran ahead of him, out into the empty street. It was just after noon and almost every *Weeklundian* was missing, confined somewhere within their own span of memnesia. The whole neighborhood was completely quiet except for the sound of a car's engine idling across the street, its windows darkly tinted.

12

The Stop

"Frank, you'll never guess what I just saw."

Frank recognized Curt's voice and replied, "I told you never to call me directly. How did you get my number?"

"Yuri gave it to me."

He relented a little, still angry inside. "So, get to the point and keep it short. We've had indications that they're trying to tap us again," Frank barked.

"OK, well about fifteen minutes ago I was parked across from that detective's house. You know, the one I've been checking on, the former partner of Warren Wheaton."

"So?"

"So, he and his dog walked right by me!" Curt was sure his news would be really important. He thought it should have elicited more than a simple "So?"

"So what?" Frank barked again.

"Well, do you know what day of the week that this guy always has his loss of memory?"

"No I don't, but apparently you do. Get on with it."

"Yes I do and it's today!" He heard a gasp at the

other end of the line followed by silence. "Either he's not from *Weeklun,* we've got the wrong man, or he's found some way to bypass the effects," said Curt with an air of triumph in his voice.

Frank's mind was racing. "It's got to be a mistake. Curt got his facts mixed up. It really wasn't William what's his name... must have been somebody else." In spite of his confusion he knew what he had to do.

Finally, he said in his powerful yet lowered voice, "You're off the case from now on. You'll receive your pay in the mail. Good bye!" Frank just hung up-no thanks for the fine work he did, no promise of possible future work, not even a grunt of acknowledgement.

Curt had just been fired and hung up on at the same time. He was more than peeved at being treated that way. "If I ever get my hands on that guy I'll...," he fumed as he punched his own 'hang-up' button. He didn't know why but he stayed parked across from William's house a little longer.

. . .

Meanwhile, William and Granville finished their neighborhood walk and had returned home by twelve forty-five. They had walked many blocks throughout their neighborhood and returned from a different direct-ion. He closed the front door and plopped down on the living room couch. He was elated. He hadn't felt any drowsiness or disruption of thought at all. He could also remember everything! In fact, it seemed to him that his perceptions were even more acute than normal. His experiment had actually worked! Then, suddenly from out of nowhere, he remembered having heard an engine idling from that non-descript maroon sedan that he noticed sitting across the street, the one he and Granville had walked by. He remembered it very clearly because it was so quiet everywhere else. It was the only noise there was. It seemed out of place. "Why would anyone sit in their car and leave the engine running during their period of memnesia? That doesn't make any sense." he thought. He quickly got up and peeked out between the blinds. The car was still there.

"I don't feel good about this," he thought as his pulse began to race. His detective training had slipped into gear. He ran to his bedroom where he had a pair of binoculars and ran back. He would try to get its license plate number. Just as he slowly pulled his blinds back he saw the car begin to move forward. He looked through his binoculars at the now enlarged image of its bumper and could see no license plate at all! Now he was fully alert. He jotted down all of the car's description that he could and then dialed the police department's number.

"Hello. You've reached the Morristown Police Department. In order to help us improve our services to you this call may be recorded. Due to circumstances beyond our control there is no one here to take your call. But, if you wish to leave a number for us to call you back press "one". Someone will contact you as soon as possible. If you know the extension of the person you're trying to reach enter it now followed by the pound key. If you want to leave a voice message and know the extension of that person please press "two" and you will be offered other directions at that time... Otherwise please remain on the line and someone will take your call in the order we have received them. Thank you for your patience."

"The maroon car has travelled a quarter of a mile during that blasted recording," he thought to himself as he continued to wait, "That's no way to run an emergency police call line particularly on a Saturday." He waited patiently for four more long rings and then hung up in utter frustration.

He looked down a Granville and said, "Well, maybe going out for a walk wasn't so smart an idea after all. I think we'd better drive over to the station. Come on pal I need some companionship."

They arrived at the station only twelve minutes later because of the almost complete reduction of noontime traffic. It was one of the few benefits of being a *Weeklundian* around that time of day. As they entered the lobby side by side, he greeted the weekend duty officer, "Hi Don. How are you doin' today?"

Don was on the phone and only smiled, waved quickly in response and then continued writing something in his huge call book. He never noticed Granville who was out of sight well below his tall lectern.

William and his trusty companion raced to the chief's office but, when they got there, the lights were off and the door closed. "Dang," he murmured. Then he turned around and ran upstairs to his office with Granville panting close behind. As he entered, he saw another youngish-looking detective he didn't know very well-a new hire. "Hi, the name's William Thomas," he said.

The other man smiled and extended his arm to shake hands as he replied, "Yeah, I've seen you around. I'm Rick Mancardo."

"Can I use your computer? Mine's turned off over the weekend... hackers you know."

"Sure, be my guest," Rick answered. "Can I help?"

William just replied, "Not yet at least. I've got to track down a two-door maroon sedan with no rear plate that was casing my home about fifteen minutes ago.

Rick gave him a funny look as if to say, "It's supposed to be the other way around isn't it?" but he didn't.

William quickly typed in an "*All-Points Bulletin*" describing the automobile as best he could. It flashed out to every police cruiser and officers' cell phone in Morristown and surrounds. Unfortunately, the message employed an extremely low-level encryption due to limited department funds. Unbeknownst to William and the rest of the department most of the wealthier criminals had long-since hacked the algorithm and were able to stay a little ahead of the law because of it. They all smiled smugly as they read William's message on their cell phones and laptops; most of them were left wondering what that alert was about.

. . .

Another laptop was open and sitting on the seat beside Curt who was at the city's limit by now and travelling southeast in the direction of *Yurland* exactly at the posted speed limit. He had programmed his computer to ring a bell and flash the screen three times whenever any police message alerts came through.

"What's that?" he muttered. He glanced down at the open screen beside him but the angle was wrong and the type way too small for his aging eyes. He would have to pull over. He was angry that his eyes weren't as young as they used to be.

Just as he began to find a place to pull over onto the shoulder a sheriff passed him in the opposite direction on the four-lane highway. The sheriff looked back at the car in his rear-view mirror and wondered if he needed assistance. Then he noticed that the driver who was now over on the shoulder hadn't turned on his emergency flashers as he should have. "I'd better give him some cover and warn him about the fine if he ever does it again;" he waited for a break in the oncoming traffic and then did a sharp U turn several hundred yards beyond Curt's car. Curt hadn't noticed him because he had been trying to see who the incoming police message was from and what it said.

Curt set his brake and put the car's transmission into park and then rotated the computer screen to face him. He was looking down and unaware of the other traffic.

Just as the words on the screen began to enter his consciousness, he looked up and noticed the reflection of the bright yellow emergency lights flashing on the roof of the sheriff's car. It had pulled in right behind him! Curt could see him in both of his mirrors.

"Oh crap," he cried and quickly went through several of his pre-planned feint routines in his mind. He knew he was very good at them. Just the thought gave him self-confidence. He could also shoot it out with him but the sheriff had the positional advantage, he realized. "Don't over-react," he told himself, "stay calm."

The Sheriff sat there motionless as he routinely radioed in his stop. Then he noticed that there was no license plate on the car. His anxiety level went up several notches. "Control, this is Sheriff Hunter. I'm on route 234 about nine miles west of the *Weeklun-Yurland* border. I need backup," he began. He gave a short description of the car ahead of him.

"This is Control. You're comin' loud and clear. You need to know that we've just received an "*All-Points*" from the *Weeklun* Police Department in Morristown to be on the lookout for that car. Be advised that the occupant or occupants may be armed and dangerous. Do you copy that?"

The sheriff acknowledged the message and said, "I'm going to investigate... but get some back up here if you can. Signing out."

Meanwhile, Curt had decided to play it cool and draw upon his well-refined skills at deception. He saw the Sheriff get out of his car slowly, leaving the car door open, "not a good sign," but he was relieved when he saw that there wasn't another deputy with him. "One-on-one," he thought, "pretty fair odds." Curt quickly closed his laptop, grabbed a rumpled soiled broad-brimmed canvas fishing hat from the seat beside him and jammed it on his head. Then he conjured up his best fishin' story. "This had better be good," he mumbled out loud. At the same time, he took his semi-automatic pistol from his shoulder holster and put it out of sight under the front seat where he could reach it quickly. He didn't have time to take off his leather holster and its straps. If he were patted down, he would have more than a fish story to make up.

He watched the Sheriff approaching his side of the car in his rear-view mirror. He seemed to be walking very slowly and had his right hand sitting on the top of his gun, "not good." But it was still in its holster, "better." Curt knew he had no record at all, no warrants out for him, "good." But he also knew that he had taken the rear plate off for this job, "really a stupid thing to do." He waited patiently as he placed both hands in plain sight on the top of his steering wheel. "That might help him drop his guard a little," he thought.

"Sir. I want you to open your window... that's far enough. Now, please get out of your car and keep your hands where I can see them. Move slowly."

Curt followed his orders very precisely except that his hands were now shaking. As he climbed out he accentuated a limp in his right leg. He bent forward as if he had painful arthritis. It made him look much shorter and older than he was; he moved even more slowly than the sheriff had ordered-molasses in the winter moved faster. "So, what's wrong officer?" he croaked with a beautifully orchestrated weakness in the voice of an old man.

"I'm sorry sir, but your car has no license plate in the rear. Can you explain that?"

Curt's spirit soared. "That was the reason he stopped me," he thought to himself," he doesn't know anything else."

"Well officer, I'm... I'm awful sorry 'bout that... been meanin' to fix it on for several days now... it's back at the house in the garage... I sure hope that it isn't that important." He said in a slow southern *Weeklun* drawl. Silently he said to himself, "Let's see if that does it. If it doesn't we'll just have to ramp it up to the next level."

"Well sir, Let's begin by seeing your driver's license."

As Curt slowly reached back for his wallet he winced as if he was in pain. He gave his head a slight sideways tremor. He was putting on a great act. Finally, he fumbled his wallet out and said, "Can I use both hands officer, to get it out?"

The sheriff dropped his guard even more. "This old gent isn't armed or dangerous. He's probably wetting his pants right now," He thought. Out loud he said, "Yes, please take it out and hand it to me."

Curt did. His hands were still shaking.

Sheriff Hunter looked at the name, age, address and color photo of the driver and said, “Please wait here, sir. I’ll be right back.” He returned to his cruiser and called in the number on the card (His name was Curtis O. Schneider) along with other information such as his age which clearly wasn’t as old as he had been acting. He waited several minutes for their reply, “no outstanding warrants, no weapons permit, no driving violations… he’s clean… advise when he’s released.” He relaxed a little more but asked, “…then why is there an all-points bulletin out on the car?” When he got no answer he just replied, “Roger that, over and out.” Then he began walking back toward the man standing shivering beside his car.

Just about then a state patrol car arrived and pulled in behind Hunter’s cruiser, its intense flashing lights adding even more illumination over the entire area. Curt turned and saw him and said “Oh no. I’m really in deep trouble now.”

Five minutes later his hands were handcuffed behind him and he was sitting in the back seat of the Sheriff’s car. He was still wearing his shoulder holster. They had discovered it but hadn’t taken it off of him. His gun was impounded. He was also muttering something about false arrest but he had suddenly lost his accent.

“Thanks Sheriff. Very good work. Could you bring him in to our main station?” the Morristown police operator said.

. . .

Meanwhile, several hundred miles to the southeast, Frank was getting ready to drive to Morristown. He had that feeling that only happens when you know you're holding a full house. Because of the phone call he knew he was onto something really big. Actually, it was Curt who had stumbled onto perhaps the biggest break-through any criminal could ever ask for: a way to even the score, to be free from memnesia while the law was helpless, at least for certain periods of time! There couldn't be anything much better than that for business," he thought with a smile. "It doesn't matter that Curt did it. If I can play it right it's all mine now," he said to himself. "And maybe I can lease it out for big, really big money." His mind rapidly expanded to the national level; armies could invade almost at will, stock brokers could control markets, certain businesses could topple others by controlling the "right timing," and even national productivity could be controlled. He was becoming even more excited. "The applications are endless. Only, I have to be certain!"

Frank prided himself on being both systematic and very well read. "They're two of the reasons I'm so successful... I learned long ago that if one holds any contempt about anything before even investigating it it can block all further information and progress. It may keep *Memlandians* in everlasting ignorance but I'm not going to be one of them!" he said to himself in a burst of pride. It was one of his most favorite mantras.

His brand-new sports car had carried him to Morristown quickly and smoothly in a little under four hours. It had been a relaxing trip for it gave him time to rehearse his story to detective William Thomas or anyone else who might ask: "I'm a business-man from *Yurland*, a rare book dealer who also knows a number of ancient languages. I'm looking for new books to buy for my many wealthy clients around *Mem*." That should be a sufficient story if it's needed. Frank knew that he could make the rest up on the spot if it was necessary. He prided himself on a keen intellect and great imagination. He also realized that his plan would take time, effort and money to pull it off.

He arrived early in the evening and booked in to one of the most expensive hotels in the city. He enjoyed its bar followed by its elegant dining facilities and finally its specially-designed prestige cigar-smoking 'Man-Cave.' In fact, that was its name. It possessed negative air pressure yet was said to be hermetically sealed, had polished walnut paneling, ultra-soft leather sofas, huge marble ash trays, and a beautifully crafted stone fireplace with a welcoming flickering fire burning real wood. In addition, several handsome men in tuxedoes made certain everyone was supplied with whatever drinks they wanted.

Somehow its many fragrant odors had snuck out into the hallway to lure men (and some women) inside. He wasn't a member of the exclusive smoker's club but when he pulled out two hundred currency notes it bought him one evening's "guest" membership without any delay at all.

Everything there made him feel relaxed and right at home. The only others present were three other men sitting together across the room. He kept an eye on them but they never showed him any interest as far as he could tell.

His cigar was the most expensive, a Belicosos, a hefty five and one-half inches long and over eight-tenths of an inch in diameter, a ring gauge of 52. He ordered a snifter of cognac to go along with it, the kind of drink that, when ordered where others can overhear, raises eyebrows and swivels heads: "rancio on top of rancio-guadruple rancio," "at least sixty years in the cask," "over forty-six ABV." "the smoothest eaux-de-vie you have." Frank knew his cognac. As he was leaving almost an hour later he bought himself a whole bottle. It cost him just under four hundred notes and he carried it out of the restaurant and up to his room as conspicuously as he could.

. . .

At the same time William was at the police station "Interviewing" Curt. Every word was captured on tape. It was getting late and he knew he couldn't hold him very long-the charges were very weak, right on the edge of falling through.

"All right Mr. Schneider. We know that you're anxious to get home to your family, if you've got one, so I'll get right to the point. What were you doing outside my house this morning? We know it was you."

Curt sat mute and immobile yet his eyes were laughing back at William because he knew they had absolutely nothing solid on him. He would be free in hours or less... he wouldn't even need an attorney! He could play with them and have fun. The first words out of his mouth were, "So's there some law here against parking against a curb?"

William exchanged glances with the officer who was standing by the door and then went on, "Let me put it this way. Isn't it a little strange that a visitor to my neighborhood who is wearing a firearm, which is against the law here without a special permit and which I might add you don't have, would be watching my house? Doesn't that sound a little strange to you?"

"You can't prove I was looking at anyone's house. You know as well as I do that my windows are so dark you couldn't see where I was looking. How do you know I wasn't making a cell call and had just pulled over trying to be a safe citizen?"

William knew he was right. It was the beginning of the end of his interrogation. All they had on the man was unlawful possession of a firearm, no license plate and maybe not turning his emergency flashers on, nothing else. Pretty weak. "But at least it will give him a record, William thought with some satisfaction. "It might even keep him off his street as well."

"Why were you carrying a firearm at all?" It was a logical question that William knew he had to ask.

"It's for my protection," he replied with a smirk on his creased and lopsided face.

"And what kind of protection would you need? You look like a guy in good shape, the kind that could take care of anyone giving you trouble." "It never hurts to build up a little self-pride," William thought to himself.

Curt fell for it and said, "You're right there for a change. I can take care of myself if I have to," then he abruptly shut up again.

William needed more information about the man. He finally said, "Well, Mr. Schneider, can you tell us where you were born and grew up? We can find out, along with lot of other things, but you can save us all some time."

Curt sat silently, trying to out-wait the detective's patience. He only smirked and squinted, his eyes staring down at the table top. "I'm the master here. There is no way they can force me," he thought to himself smugly.

William tried a different approach. “Isn’t it odd that someone like you feels so insecure that he has to be armed?”

“What do you mean by someone like you?” Curt exclaimed. “What are you saying?” He felt personally insulted and wanted to know just what the detective meant.

William waited to see if he was going to saying anything else. When he didn’t William went on, “What I’m saying is that law abiding citizens don’t carry weapons around… so why do you… if you’re just a normal law-abiding citizen as you want us to believe?”

Curt answered, “’cause some time ago I was robbed at gun point and I decided to not ever let it happen again.”

That was the opening that William was waiting for. He said, “I’m sorry to hear that. Did they get very much?

“Yeh, a lot of money and all my wallet cards and ID. They were the hardest to replace.”

“I can imagine,” he replied trying to sound sympathetic. “It’s a lot of work to cancel the card accounts and reset all those passwords… Oh, by the way, how much money did you lose?”

He blurted out without thinking, “About two grand.” He suddenly realized he shouldn’t have said that and shut up again, his face reddening.

William went on without showing any emotion, “So you bought a pistol in case it ever happened again.”

Curt thought to himself, “Well, that’s a reasonable question” and answered, “Sure”.

“Just where did you buy it Mr. Schneider?”

He didn’t answer.

"You know that we can trace it. Every firearm has a record of one kind or another trailing behind it."

Again, Curt remained silent.

"Mr. Schneider, you know, your silence tells us a lot about you. It says that you're covering something up. Now, let's try again, Where did you purchase your weapon?"

Finally Curt answered hesitantly, "At a gun shop in *Yurland.*"

"Exactly where in *Yurland*?"

"The south side of Elton. I don't remember its name."

"Thank you sir. Now let's proceed to that two thousand you said you lost. Did you ever get it back?" (What William didn't know was that Curt had actually stolen the money from someone else using his gun for persuasion).

Curt smiled a moment as he remembered his night-time robbery on that dark street on Elton's affluent side. He really needed the money because he was on his way to a poker game with Frank and some other associates. He replied smugly, "Well, yes I did but it was in a card game the same night. I used my hidden fifty and won twenty five hundred... it was a pretty good night."

"And where was this game?"

Curt thought to himself, "Where is this going? What does it matter where the game was?" He decided to make up an answer, "It was in a warehouse down by the rail yard. That's all I can remember."

"So you won your money back... pretty lucky night I'd say."

"You bet it was. I'd like to be robbed every night if they could all end that way."

William smiled and nodded for a moment at his

answer. Curt seemed to be more relaxed now and talkative which was good. Then William asked, "And can you remember the names of any of the people you played with that night? Were there any women there?" It was an old ploy-to insert an irrelevant detail to distract the suspect long enough to interrupt his defensive answers.

Curt cried, "What a stupid thing to ask. No! There weren't any women there! When they play they play dirty." He frowned and pursed his lips together as he recalled something from the past. William watched him carefully. Then Curt added without thinking, "It was a long time ago... the only name I think I can remember was a Frank somebody... so why's that important?"

"Well, it may be or it may not be. Let me go on. "Do you consider yourself a good poker player?"

Curt smiled again for he liked this kind of question. It gave him an opportunity to brag. "Yeah, I guess I do. I've been able to buy a few bottles of decent cognac in my time from my winnings?"

William's eye brows shot up. "Where have I heard that term before?" he thought. He was puzzled. "It's unusual for someone who has all the characteristics of an underworld type to be drinking cognac. I wonder whether that's a detail that might be valuable later on?" William followed the lead. "So, you like cognac. That's interesting. I bet you know a lot about it, how it's made, what the best brands are, where to get it at a good price?"

Curt acted suspicious. His questions didn't seem to be related to anything. He only said, "Well I know enough to buy the best." He was boasting again. He couldn't help it.

"And what is the best in your opinion?" William asked.

“It’s rancio and well-aged if that’s anything to you,” he replied. He thought to himself, “I’ll bet he’s never even tasted cognac.”

The interview was concluded: Curt was booked: it included his fingerprints, mug-shot, and a filled-out person-of-interest processing sheet; he spent the rest of the night in a jail cell; amazingly, it was the first time in his life. The whole experience did a lot of damage to his self-image for he had always believed he was a man who couldn’t get caught. Now he realized he would have to face a court hearing and his new-found record would reduce his prestige in the eyes of future employers as well as the amount of money he could extort from them for his services. At the same time, he was certain he would be acquitted.

The next morning he left the police station a somewhat different man, not necessarily defeated but more deflated. He knew that he would need to sharpen up his act.

13

Pages Speak Again

It was Sunday morning. William had had a stressful Saturday but he slept soundly until Granville woke him at quarter past seven. He needed to go outside again. William let him out and finished washing and dressing and then ate a light breakfast. He wasn't hungry at all for some reason. He checked through the front drapes and frowned when he saw Granville digging in the neighbor's yard again. He whistled and his furry companion rushed back across the lawn and bounded inside again shivering from the cold morning air. His wet feet left tracks on the bare wood floor.

William wanted to wind down today. He even tried to put the wondrous results of yesterday's "faith experiment" out of his mind for a while. And while he still felt secure inside his house, he couldn't help himself. He kept getting up and looking out the window at the nearly empty street out front. An occasional car or truck would pass by and he would watch them just to make sure they didn't stop or slow down. Each one brought a slight twinge of anxiety that someone might be watching him. "I'm not afraid," he thought to himself. Then he smiled and looked down at Granville and said, "Well, you big mut, we've got each other, don't we? You're my trusty watch dog, at least you do a whole lot of watching." The two exchanged grins.

As eight a.m. approached, he decided to get the little book out again from where he had hidden it the night before. He wanted to go over the part again about what one had to do to overcome one's memnesia. He wondered whether the steps would have to be followed every time or could there be a simpler, more convenient way? It could make a huge difference in whether it would be accepted and applied by the masses. Once again, he got up and glanced out the window. He realized that his window was going to be a definite distraction from now on so he simply closed the front drapes as if doing so would solve the problem.

While he had copied down all of the margin notes he couldn't remember them all. So it was on page one hundred fifty-four, penned carefully in jet black ink, that he read almost for the first time:

"If faith is sure it's effect is forever"

"Could that be the answer to my question?" he asked himself. "It might be, it does make some sense." He read on trying to see if there were other clues that might answer his question.

Just as had happened the night before, when he first opened the book, the pages were simply smooth white paper. Nothing was visible on them except the inked margin notes. "That is its normal, its default state without faith present," he reasoned. "And I'll bet that's part of the answer to my question. The *Secret of Mem* must be coaxed out of its protective normal state. It's not meant just for everyone!" His sudden revelation sent shivers of electrical shock through him. "This wondrous book must somehow be self-protective, responding deliberately to protect the people of *Mem* from others who would misuse its teachings. Maybe it even realizes its own power to be used for good or evil! If this is true it means that it must have a consciousness of its own!" More shivers exploded through him. The implications were enormous. It violated absolutely every scientific principle he had ever read or heard about.

As he calmed down and focused his mind back to the invisible text once again, he concentrated hard and allowed the thought - "I believe, I really do believe" - to enter his mind. As he did so the words appeared-faintly at first and then darker and darker in proportion to how much he truly believed that they would appear. As he had surmised each page seemed to be able to read the genuineness of his spirit and respond appropriately; was he controlling them or were they acting to reinforce his own faith like some psychological conditioning experiment in a laboratory?

He was gradually coming to see that the fantastic *Secret of Mem* that these magical pages offered should not be shared with everyone on the planet... particularly with people like Curt, for example! He was contemplating this question when the same voice as before suddenly broke into his thoughts:

"And which kind are you?"

William looked down at Granville for some kind of confirmation of the reality of the voice but, as before, he gave none. "There's that voice in my head again," he said. "Am I talking to myself? But he's been right so far. I'd better listen."

Deep down William knew what the voice was really asking. He had to be honest with himself and face the question of whether even he was worthy of knowing the secret and benefiting from it? As he tossed this question back and forth, he realized that the little book had opened itself to him again, it had tested his own faith, as weak as he knew it was. "Isn't that all the proof I need? If the little book has accepted me, shouldn't I?" He asked. "But do I have the right to share its truths with anyone else? And if so with whom?"

"What if I told Wini about the book? How would she react if I showed it to her? Would she even be able to see anything on the page? She'd think I was crazy. And what about the chief?" As his mind began to whirr the text faded out again. "I've got to stay focused!" he said out loud.

Granville must have agreed for he raised his head and gave a quiet woof in reply. William looked at him and laughed. "Thanks buddy, I needed that." William sat there mute for a long time pondering the decision he faced.

"I guess the idea of showing the book to others might make some sense. Many people would not only gain because they have more productive hours during the day but, more importantly, there had to be other benefits when they realized that their faith has real power," he reasoned. "If I let the secret out selectively it would be a kind of controlled experiment. It wouldn't only test the genuineness of their faith but, if the text did show up for them, it would also prove that I'm not insane... proof of my sanity in exchange for proof of their faith, what a tradeoff!"

Yet still, he was afraid of being laughed at if he did show the book to anyone else and all they could see was blank paper. They would say, "you're out of your mind," "the whole idea is "preposterous," "William, you're ready for the asylum." Just for a moment, as he began to doubt its reality again, he watched in fascination as the text began to fade away. "No! I'm not going to tell anyone, at least not yet. But what else can I do with it except become its caretaker, its custodian, while I'm alive." (Warren had concluded the same thing and had joined the myriad others who had accepted the same sacred trust before him). William finally began to realize it would be a gigantic responsibility. He set the little book down again and sat back wondering what he would do.

. . .

His first stop the next morning was at a large commercial real estate office in downtown Morristown where he signed up to rent a ground-floor run-down brick office space for six months. Frank paid the security deposit and the first two-month's rent in advance in cash. He was surprised and pleased by how fast the paperwork had gone through because of his wad of fresh crisp new paper currency. By two p.m. he had placed a modest-sized but prominent newspaper ad for his *Rare and Antique Book Finders-Ltd.* bookstore. The four-inch column ad included several carefully planned lies. His firm would *'buy and sell all kinds of books, manuscripts and other printed material'* that, in his own "expert judgement," were valuable. The newspaper's ad department never asked for proof of any of the details. The ad also included his address and business hours. The one thing he didn't do was apply for a city business license (He had used an alias and forged I.D. documents for all his other transactions and knew he would be long gone before the city discovered their loss). Then he contacted his staff back in *Yurland* to ship him five hundred of his oldest books as soon as possible. By the time they arrived two days later in one of his "delivery trucks" he had had old second-hand stained wooden shelves installed in his long gloomy narrow space. Two shelves with his oldest books arrayed on them faced the street and could be seen and admired through the shop's two small discrete plate glass windows. It was really beginning to look like he had been in business for years. His only signage onto the street was a carefully hand-lettered sign made to look old and weathered even though it was brand new (It was painstakingly rendered by a forger who owed him from the past). He hung the quaint and understated sign at eye level beside the narrow entry door. On his polished antique walnut desk, he placed a family picture of a beautiful middle-aged woman with two college-age children standing beside her and smiling. They were in a lavish back yard; they were his "borrowed family" from one of his employees back in *Yurland.* Sitting beside the photograph was his unopened bottle of cognac. He wanted to impress his customers with his fine ultra-expensive tastes. He had also gone to a do-it-yourself print shop and made two hundred fifty business cards-all by himself. All they said was *Antique Books and Manuscripts*, his name, address and phone number in an antique looking font. He was almost in business!

He looked around the place four days after he moved in and smiled. He was extremely proud of himself; he was now a businessman. Then he simply waited for his trap to do its work.

. . .

William was feeding Grandville his morning breakfast the next day when his phone range. It was Wini.

"Hello William, this is Wini," she began. "How are you?"

"I am keeping pretty busy thanks, and you?"

"Me too. I hope I haven't called at a bad time."

"No. I'm just feeding Granville but he can wait, I think," he replied with a laugh.

Wini also laughed and said, "What kind of dog is he?"

"A golden lab, about as cute and fluffy as you could want. I've had him for… let me see, about four years now. He's been my faithful companion here. He's my official watchdog. Yeh… all he ever does is lie around and watch," he said with another laugh.

"How wonderful to have someone to come home to," she replied and then she choked up. In the silence that followed he knew she was crying. She finally got ahold of herself and continued, "I'm just calling to see if you've made any progress in you know what?" She was referring to the page with notes she had found in Warren's hiking jacket that she had given him.

He answered, "Well, not really, but I'm not someone who gives up easily." (He knew he had to lie for he couldn't tell her anything about the black book).

"I know that William. Oh, and by the way, I've been searching through the house for anything else here besides that piece of paper I gave you and so far I've only come across one more thing. I don't know if it's important."

"Oh? What was it?"

"Well I found it in one of his desk drawers in a small metal box that he used to keep his spare change in. It was a white card, the kind you keep recipes on, about two and a half by four inches. Warren had printed some words on it in black ink, very precisely for some reason."

William strained forward waiting.

"You know what he wrote?" she said, it was "You can only see it if you have faith that it is there." He had underlined the word faith. It doesn't make any sense to me."

William took a quick breath and stood frozen for a moment. He knew where he had heard those same words before-it was that voice that came from out of nowhere or maybe it was just his own mind. But he was absolutely sure they weren't any words handwritten on any piece of paper he had seen! "That kind of coincidence just can't happen," he thought. "That voice must have spoken to Warren as well!" The pieces of the puzzle were slowly starting to fit together. "Warren must have known the *Secret of Mem* and had been applying its teachings just as I'm doing." He didn't share any of his conjecture with Wini.

This confirmation gave him renewed confidence that he was on the right track. He was getting excited and tried not to let it show, "Thanks Wini. That might be another piece of the puzzle... or not."

"Well, I hope so. I hope it means something to you, it sure doesn't to me."

William needed to change the subject and interjected, "Wini, I just remembered, I did come across something in Warren's files that was in a language I couldn't read (He didn't tell her that it came from the little book itself). I have no idea what it says. Do you know somebody who is into ancient *Memlandian* languages?

"What a coincidence, William! I was reading the newspaper yesterday and I noticed an ad for a rare book dealer in Morristown who said he also knew ancient *Memlandian* languages. I don't know why I'd remember something like that... but he might be able to help you."

Instantly more questions flashed through his mind, "Should I risk showing him the book? Would he be able to read it at all? Could he really translate the text and, if he could, would they make any sense? Could he be trusted with knowing the *Secret of Mem*?" He finally spoke, "Hey that's great, Wini. Could you give me the address and phone number?"

. . .

It was Saturday morning around eleven-forty-five when Frank sauntered casually down the sidewalk on the opposite side of the street from William's small white-frame house. He wanted to check out what kind of place he lived in and the neighborhood, maybe even see for himself what Curt had seen at noon. Frank needed to be sure himself. He had closed his shop down town for several hours.

He had his spiel rehearsed in case he needed it: business man, looking for a home to buy or rent in the neighborhood, job change, going to move his family here soon, sizing it up for his wife... of eighteen years, by the way, I'm in the rare books business. He thought he was ready. (What Frank didn't know was that William was still as paranoid about the traffic and passers-by as he had been the week before. Almost every loud passing truck lifted him up off his couch to run over and peer out the window, binoculars in one hand, notepad in the other). He happened to be looking out the window when Frank was approaching across the street.

He had never seen the man before: tall, muscular,

and quite athletic; wearing dark blue slacks and a white polo sweater over a shirt and tie, obviously well-groomed and rich. "Maybe he's just a new neighbor out for a walk," he thought. "He doesn't look suspicious other than being so dressed up for a weekend. He's probably a real estate agent. If he's a *Daytunian* he should know that he'll soon be going into his time of memnesia. He's sure looking over here a lot." By the time William thought to look at the stranger through his binoculars he had passed and all he could see was the left-rear side of his head and dark brown hair, it was long but clearly cut and groomed by a professional.

At that same moment Frank happened to turn around quickly and glance across at William's front porch and picture window. He noticed the curtains part a little and then close again quickly. "I hope he didn't see me," he thought to himself. Then he continued walking on until he was out of sight.

Even though William wanted to return to his study of the little book he had a funny feeling about that man. He seemed out of place for some reason. But he knew he couldn't let one stranger rearrange his whole day so he returned to his task. William wanted to try out the memnesia *Cure* on himself a second time. It had actually worked the week before and had left a lingering sense of expectancy inside him all week long.

As the minute hand of his watch finally approached noon he didn't even open the book this time but only concentrated his mind on what he remembered it had instructed about *The Cure*. "If it works, I probably won't even need the book anymore," he thought.

His blood pressure and pulse were both increasing slowly because his subconscious, conditioned over a lifetime, knew that noon was approaching and the day of the week was right. But, to his utter amazement and joy, he remained wide awake for the next eleven minutes looking back and forth at his watch and all around the room in order to remember the smallest detail. He wanted to make sure he was really awake the whole time. Granville sensed that something unusual was happening and came over to sit beside him the whole time. "What a real friend you are," William thought as he patted his head. "I'll remember you more than anything else today."

After his usual span of missing time had passed William realized *The Cure* really worked! He was set free from what everyone else was coping with in *Weeklun* as well as everyone else on the whole planet during their own times of oblivion. As he digested this awesome fact, he felt elated. It was like nothing he had ever experienced before. It was more than joy and peace, far more than refreshing; he felt like he was a brand-new man, a peacefully contented man. "And it all happened because of my faith... and of course this little black book." He marveled.

He discovered that he could use the rest of the day more efficiently than he ever had before. Somehow, his mind seemed sharper and more firmly focused than ever, his memory was even clearer. He picked up the little book again and continued reading.

He was fascinated to learn about the many consequences of memnesia that were discussed in the last section of the book. Some of them were obvious; for example, that events that happened during one's time of memnesia couldn't be documented because they weren't remembered. They all became non-events. This led to many kinds of practical problems such as injuring oneself during hunting trips or getting lost on hikes during one's time of forgetfulness. One might not seek first aid if one never remembered getting hurt. One might also have no firm evidence for legal support later.

The book also mentioned that early studies had been equivocal about whether the body gained any actual physical or mental restorative power during sleep much less periods of memnesia? Everyone had just presumed that the two produced the same physiological effects but this had never been proven. But now William knew differently. He had experienced the awesome and almost sudden change in himself. He had remained fully alert during a period when, before, he had become a prisoner of noon. He knew that his personal experience wasn't any kind of scientific proof yet he couldn't get the idea and the hope out of his mind that the effect was universal. (This hope would become one of the predominant determiners of his ultimate decision).

As he read on he arrived at the other end of the spectrum of consequences: national defense and war.

A nation whose citizenry was asleep around noon every day or even once a week would be far more weakened and vulnerable to invasion than, say in *Yurland* where each citizen faced it only once a year! A grade school student could understand that. *Yurland's* solders could be selected purely on the basis of the date of the end of their prolonged memnesia and, if the conflict lasted longer than a year, when their time for memnesia came again, they could be replaced by others who had just emerged and had a full year ahead of them.

William quickly came to see that telling all *Memlandians* how to overcome their cognitive challenge could work either way, either increase or reduce the chance of war.

The book went on to discuss a wide range of other issues related to public education. Without careful scheduling how could school teachers and college professors be expected to educate students efficiently if everyone was forced to take a siesta of differing durations on different days? One student might become comatose for fifteen minutes around noon while another would be "out" for hours or longer? What a terrible waste of time it would be for everyone! Scheduling these classes would be a nightmare.

William had never thought about issues like these before, issues that memnesia had forced upon many millions of people. And, like everyone else, he had just accepted the loss of time and memory as a normal part of life... until now!

To many *Memlandians* their missing time and memory had become an idol of sorts, a wasteful, controlling, useless, passive idol. The more he thought about its invisible absolute tyranny the angrier he got. He cried out, "It's not fair! Memnesia isn't fair! It's given a tremendous benefit to *Yurlandians* and not to the rest of us."

As he weighed one side of his decision against the other one question kept coming back to him. "If every one of the earlier custodians of this book had known about these positive consequences of disclosing the secret why hadn't any of them done it? Their decisions had all been the same. Every one of them had kept the secret, generation after generation. Their margin notes had not countermanded their logic nor disclosed their reasons. What did they know that he didn't?

He spent the rest of the day pondering what his decision would be.

14

The Next Day

"For now at least I don't think I'll let anyone know about the book or see it," William thought as he climbed out of bed the next morning. The decision had come to him during his sleep, morphing into his plan for the near future. He thought it probably was the right decision.

He had had a great rest and attributed it to what he had experienced during the time of his *Cure* the day before. In fact, he even associated his increasingly positive attitude toward life with the teachings in the book. "If only I had known about them earlier in my life," he thought. The mysterious black, leather-bound book was becoming almost religious to him, something far more than valuable, it was offering him truly lasting, life-giving joy and peace deep down inside.

It was Sunday, his day off. But he knew it could quickly turn into some kind of disaster. Life had a way of doing that. He knew that his study of the little book wasn't over yet even though he had successfully learned what the *Secret of Mem* was. His main objective for the day was to figure out how he was going to get the difficult passages in the book translated, or at least better understood, without disclosing their source. He had started formulating his plan just as he had drifted off to sleep the night before.

He let Granville out again, washed, dressed, and ate his usual quick minimally nutritious "guys' breakfast" and then dug the book out again from its hiding place. He knew from his detective training and on the job experience that any half-proficient thief would have found it in a matter of minutes and so he slept with the door blocked again, his guard dog on duty and his weapon within quick reach.

It was ten o'clock before he dialed the chief's home number and, after many rings finally heard his voice, "Hello. Who is this?" He was always suspicious of calls that came to his unlisted number at home.

"Hello chief, this is William. I'm sorry for disturbing you, sir, but there's something you need to know about the case I'm working on." He was deliberately vague since he had read a police memo the month before about possible phone line taps.

The chief paused. He still wasn't sure it really was William although it sounded a lot like him. His suspicion lessened when William said, "chief, I think I'm being surveilled here at home. Can we talk in private?"

The chief pursed his lips, shook his head slowly but tried to sound positive. "Sure, how about in the main city park in forty-five minutes... at the bench near the fountain?

"OK, I know the one."

"Thanks for meeting me on your day off," he said.

The chief replied, "Didn't you know that I don't get any?" He had a smile on his weathered face. (Even though William hadn't yet told his boss about finding

Warren's little book he knew he had better do it soon or it would look like he was covering up something).

First, William filled him in on the suspicious man who passed his house the day before. The chief knew about his interview with Curt at the station and the "near" false arrest that Willian might have had to answer for. He replied, "But William, just because a guy sits outside your house in his car for a while or a well-dressed man walks by your house in the middle of the day doesn't automatically make them suspicious criminals. You're not getting a little paranoid, are you?" he asked with a slight grin and raised eyebrows.

"No sir, I don't think so. But I thought it was interesting that the guy didn't freeze or fall down when noon came. He had to be from *Yurland* or maybe *Weeklun*. Why would some foreigner be walking around my neighborhood or maybe sitting so long in a car right there? I'm pretty sure there's another reason. I think I'm being targeted."

The chief studied his face intently. He knew that William was a solid detective with a proven record of picking up subtle cues-better than most in his department." What's he really trying to say?" he asked himself.

William gulped and looked down at cracks in the pavement in front of him for several seconds deciding whether or not to tell him the rest of the story. If he did it would be a major turning point in the responsibility he had unconsciously accepted as the keeper of the treasured book. At length he decided he would only tell him about the book's general characteristics and try to play it down. He had to leave out its totally unbelievable part-like its invisible text. He would only mention its margin notes. He said, "As far as Warren's book is concerned it doesn't seem to me to qualify as evidence for any crime I know of, it's more like a history book and it looks like it's very old."

"How could a blank book serve as any kind of legal evidence anyway?" he asked himself silently. He hoped the chief wouldn't ask to see the book himself. "Why would he? Still, I'd better downplay it as much as I can."

Once again he was feeling the weight of responsibility on his shoulders.

"Well sir, I didn't tell you about it last week when I finally found it because it didn't look that important, but, I think it could be the same book Warren brought back from his trip a long time ago." He waited for the explosion; he had kept this secret from his boss.

There was none.

The chief only nodded and said, "So did you find anything of importance so far, anything that might relate to Warren's change of personality or anything else related to the smuggling ring?"

At this William's face flushed and he sucked in a breath before answering. He had asked the key question and the only thing he could do now was lie.
"Well sir, I don't know yet. I need some more time and expert help to translate some parts of it and...".

The chief suddenly broke in, "Yeah, so that was what Wini Wheaton was talking about. She called me about some advertisement she had seen in the paper and that she had told you about it."

"That's right, sir, "I've been studying the little book but I kind of hit a roadblock."

"What kind of a roadblock?"

"Well, there are parts of it written in some old language that I've never seen before and she told me about a book dealer here in Morristown who says he understands ancient languages."

The chief gave him another sideways glance before finally saying, "Is that really all? What makes you think that it's worth spending any more time with the book? Why are you so focused on it? What else have you found out William?"

William knew that he would have to disclose everything sooner or later but this wasn't the time. He had to sidestep the question if he could. "Well, as I said, I've found some hand-written margin notes in it that I think could be centuries old. I understand a few of them but many others make no sense."

"What's he really trying to tell me?" the chief thought. "Margin notes... centuries old? His reasoning doesn't hang together. Maybe I need to have our staff psychiatrist talk to him or something?"

William went on. "I know this all sounds kind of crazy but Warren did come back a totally different person, didn't he?"

The chief just nodded in agreement.

"Well, I've been reading this little book myself now for a few days and I think I'm starting to feel the same way that I think he did. In fact...," he stopped for just a moment wondering if he should finally admit everything. All he could bring himself to say was, "... I'm seeing life differently now, clearer, sharper. I'm really glad to be alive. I'm seeing little details that I've been missing before this."

The chief's look of concern grew even more intense as if he were delivering a lecture to new cadets: "Detectives aren't supposed to be glad they're alive or get soft. They've got to be tough, focused, loyal, self-controlled and law abiding at all times." While he decided to let

William's comments pass he would keep a close eye on him. He turned and looked seriously in William eyes and said, "Detective, I want to know about anything you find out about the book from here on out. Is that understood?"

"Yes sir." (William didn't realize that the chief was on the verge of asking to see the book himself but something had distracted him at the last moment).

"All right. So what's your next move?"

"Well sir, I was hoping you would help me with that."

"Me? What do you have up your sleeve William?"

"Well, you see sir, I'm quite sure that there's a connection between my having this little book of Warren's and others who want it pretty badly. I think that was why people have been casing my place lately. They've probably done their homework like we have and think it contains some kind of valuable, or useful, information. But it's just a history book" (he lied). "And I also have a hunch that that antique book shop is involved in some way."

"OK, So if all that's true how does that involve me?"

"This book dealer ought to be checked out to see if he is legitimate without showing him the actual book. As far as I know, sir, he doesn't know what I look like and I'd like to keep it that way so that I can approach him myself a little later. Could you go into his shop first and ask some details about his background, the languages he is supposed to know, and if anything looks phony to you? I'll give you another old book to take in as cover. After I know more about the man, I'll be better able to plan my own visit."

The chief paused for a moment before answering. He was still ambivalent about allowing William so much time on this case that surrounded Warren's little book and not assigning him to a higher priority criminal case. He didn't have that many good men. Yet, something inside him made him say to himself, "Go on, he needs your help, it won't take you that long." So, he replied, "All right. I'll do it, get me the book. I'm very busy these days. Do you have a deadline?"

"Well the sooner the better. I don't like being the target of anonymous watchers. It's always better to be the watcher." Then he added with a grin, "I'll bring your book in to the station tomorrow morning with enough background on it for you to look like you really read it."

. . .

The next afternoon turned out to be sunny and actually warm. The wind had dropped, the air was fragrant and spring was in the air. Morristown was bustling with business including a small brand-new bookstore that fronted just off main street. Shop owners on each side of it were wondering about it since it wasn't even there a little over a week before. Something seemed fishy about it but they didn't say or do anything. *Weeklun* was a free country and people could do all kinds of strange things within the law if they wanted to.

The shop had opened at ten a.m. and had been doing a brisk business which surprised Frank. He hadn't been prepared for the three customers who had been standing outside waiting. But, they would provide him the cover of legitimacy he needed. Several gave him sideways glances as he charged them far too much or far too little for a book. "This isn't my kind of work," he mumbled to himself. "I need an assistant... I'd better get Jerome up here."

As he had expected his business fell off to nothing just as noon arrived. He decided to close up for lunch but he forgot to put up a CLOSED sign on his door. Four minutes later a tall, thin man in a gray suit walked in carrying a small book under his arm.

"Hello sir and welcome, may I help you?" Frank said with a thin smile plastered on his face, his right arm extended. He resented having to miss his lunch. "My name is Taylor, Malcomb Taylor."

The other man said, "Well I hope so. By the way, my name's Powell. You see I inherited this book from a recently deceased relative and I was wondering if it was worth anything?" holding it out toward Frank.

Frank wasn't suspicious at all. The guy was relaxed and friendly and his story made sense. He replied, "Well sir, if I may look at it a moment perhaps I can come up with a realistic value. You do want to sell it don't you?"

The chief nodded as he looked around at the many shelves of old books that seemed to fill the shop.

Frank took the book and walked over to sit down at his desk while the chief stood nearby innocently glancing around. He noticed the photograph on the desk and the unopened bottle of cognac standing beside it. "Should I comment about either one of them to this guy?" he asked himself.

Meanwhile Frank was trying to act as if he knew what he was doing. He used a large magnifying glass to inspect the inner binding, the fine characteristics of the type-set letters, the printing date. He tried to act studious and interested and only glanced up at his visitor once.

But what Frank didn't know was that William had told the chief more about the book than Frank could know through his amateur inspection. The chief could tell if he was faking it.

Finally Frank put the book back down and sat back in his chair thinking to himself, "I'm certain it's not the book I'm looking for. It's just another old book that seems to be about ancient *Memlandian* history." Then he stood up and smiled and said, "Well, Mr. Powell, it's an interesting little history published about a hundred twenty years ago but not really worth very much (he had managed to find the copyright date printed opposite the title page). "I'd say it would fetch around fifty or perhaps seventy-five in today's retail market."

"That's what I was afraid you would say," the chief replied. "It was probably not even worth bringing in."

"Oh no, sir, one never knows what real value some printed matter may have, particularly in the right market. Maps and charts are in high demand these days. I never prejudge anything. Please, always bring it in for me to look at. And now, is there anything else I can help you with?"

The chief thought for a moment and then answered, "Well perhaps there is if you can read ancient languages of *Mem*, I think almost prehistoric ones."

At this Frank's eyebrows raised in surprise as he asked, "Well that depends on many things, sir. Can you tell me a little more about the item you are referring to?"

William had supplied the chief with just enough information about Warren's book to whet Frank's appetite. He said, "Well, it's a small book quite beautyfully bound in black leather and nearly two hundred pages long. It looks like it could be very old. It has some notes written in its margins probably added much later. They are one of the things I'm interested in. Some of them are in languages that I've never seen before."

Frank was becoming more interested because this sounded like it could be the book he was looking for. He tried to keep the emotion that was rising inside him from showing. He said, "Are you interested in anything else about the book?" He realized that his probing was pretty obvious but he couldn't help himself.

"Well Mr. Taylor, to tell you the truth, there's also something kind of strange about this book. I can't even describe it very well." His vague statement was deliberate and he let it sink in.

"All right," he said. "Well, perhaps the best way to solve this is for me to inspect it. I've had years and years studying ancient history and languages."

The chief replied in as innocent a voice as he could muster, "I've had it for some time now but have been too busy to look into it... perhaps now is the time to do so, particularly if it is valuable. My wife and I could use the money."

"He's willing to sell it!" Frank thought. His heart rate increased even though he knew it might not really be the book he sought. Then he replied, "Well Mr. Powell, as I said, I'd be most willing to look at it for you. Here's my business card. If you decide you would like me to provide that service just give me a call." Frank tried to remain calm as he ushered his customer and his book out the front door. But he wasn't going to let him get away. He had to find out where he lived. He was sure that it was the book.

The chief was no fool. He had been highly trained in spotting a tail. Frank was a rank amateur and gave himself away within two blocks of his book store. He didn't turn around fast enough when the chief suddenly turned around to look behind him. He never changed his gait or his appearance by taking off his coat and slinging it over one shoulder. Frank was worse than an amateur. Just as William and the chief had planned, he led the man on across the city park where William sat slumped behind a newspaper. The chief sauntered past William with a glance and a slight nod. William waited patiently as Frank also walked by a half-minute later. "It was the same man who had cased my place last Saturday," William thought to himself. "That settles it."

After both had passed William got up and drove home and waited for his phone to ring which it did twenty minutes later.

"Hello. Did you see him?"

"Yes. That was him, the same guy walking past my house. That's quite a coincidence isn't it?" William replied. "I'd say were onto something here."

"I think you're right detective. By the way, I lost him a few minutes after we past you." There was a muted note of pride in the chief's voice. To test him the chief asked, "So, what would you suggest we do about it?"

William had thought about this question for some time and had his answer ready. "Sir, I think we should use Warren's little book, or at least a good copy of it, as bait and see what we can catch. We still don't know why they are so interested in it. And we can also look into his business license and other details to see if he is legitimate. Finally, we should tail him to see where he lives. He may turn out to be legitimate. The chief thought for a moment and then answered, "Yes. Good ideas. I'll put them in motion as soon as I get back to the station.

Oh, by the way, sir, did you notice anything unusual in his shop?"

"About his shop? Yeah, I think I did. He had a colored photograph on his desk of a good-looking woman and two children standing beside her. He wasn't in it and he wasn't wearing a wedding ring either. She looked much too young for him but maybe that's just the way things are these days. Oh, and one more thing, he had an unopened bottle of cognac sitting beside the photograph."

At hearing this William perked up, "Sir, did you say cognac? Did you notice anything at all about the bottle? It could be important." He was getting more excited.

"No, not really, it was pretty far away. But I'm sure it wasn't opened. Why would a guy set out a bottle of cognac like that except to impress his high-end clientele?"

"Yeh, why indeed?" William thought. He was disappointed that his boss hadn't been able to see anything more about the bottle. It might have linked the book store owner to Curt. Perhaps he could get another look at it himself.

. . .

Frank was angry that he lost the man when he had been forced to wait for heavy traffic to pass before crossing the street after him. He had tried twice to run across through the traffic but then thought better of it. He said, "Well, I'll just have to wait to see if he brings that book into the shop. He went back to his hotel leaving his shop unlocked with an OPEN sign hanging in the door. It wasn't any way to run a business.

. . .

It was early the next morning when William slid out

of bed and felt the icy cold floor sending its numbing shock up his legs to awaken him. As he did so he glanced over at the window; it was still dark outside. His bedside clock read five forty-five! "What woke me just now?" he wondered. Granville just yawned, stretched and went back to sleep. It was obvious that his keen ears hadn't heard anything unusual. But William was so wide awake by now that he decided to get an early start on the day. He really was changing into a brand-new man.

He finished breakfast by six-ten and was reading the little book again with help from the light of a gooseneck lamp. It was still pitch-black outside and the rest of his house lights were also dark-a perfect time to concentrate entirely on the contents of the book. He marveled yet again at how meticulously it had been organized.

It began with a concise introduction that reviewed many of the things that *Memlandians* had done to try to cure memnesia (the universal malady of the planet had no name back then and for some reason was referred to only as "The Fearful Loss").

In very ancient days when this frightening period of thoughtful nothingness and lost time had first been noticed both the *Daytunians* and the *Weeklunders* had looked for solutions that might appease their gods while calming their own fear and outrage that always rose up right around noon. They created elaborate rituals of all kinds; most of them involved repetition in one way or another; doing so seemed to enhance memory a little. And so, their dances, lyrics, prose and poetry all were thought of as terribly boring because of their almost endless repetitions.

Then a century later an elder suggested that everyone should begin their day at midnight, not noon. He had reasoned that their malady could be redefined out of existence. It couldn't. (Little did anyone realize that the problem lay not in the sun's position in the sky or the definition of a day but was buried somewhere deep within each one of them). An eon later a *Daytunian* wise man came up with a new diet. He maintained that "... our nemesis is caused by something we all eat or perhaps something we don't... some biochemical imbalance." After several decades of carefully planned and mandated national dietary supplements *Daytunians*, and other *Memlandians* who had read about the idea and tried it, finally gave up on his plan and went back to eating whatever they wanted. One unanticipated result was that increasingly they ignored advice from their dieticians.

William was fascinated as he read about another group of *Weeklundian* scientists who proposed that the length of the day should be redefined as two passages of the sun overhead. They thought that that way there would be only one period of their memnesia every two days. It, too, didn't work because so many people were unconscious during their memnesia period at noon they couldn't remember whether they were on the first or the second day of the solar zenith plan. Indeed, changing the astronomical definition hadn't solved anything either! More and more *Memlandians* began to lose confidence in pronouncements coming from their scientific community.

"How did these early primitive people come up with so many different ways to try to cure their malady?" William asked himself. He was beginning to gain a new respect for the creativity of his ancestors. Then he read about yet another "solution" in which people simply gave in to memnesia. To follow the public's lead Government leaders proclaimed a mandatory siesta for everyone at noon. This wasn't welcomed by everyone on the planet because, while every *Daytunian* might be asleep at the time, many *Weeklundians* and *Yurlanders* were not; many kinds of crimes increased significantly. "Couldn't those officials have seen that coming?" William agreed with an inked margin note beside this section of text that pronounced:

"Too much sleep is slothful, wasteful, and unnecessary."

He turned the page and read another paragraph. Then he turned to Granville who was still trying to sleep and said, "Now that's really a novel idea." Granville opened one eye, wagged his tail once and then went back to sleep. (It was still dark out and Granville almost never got up until it was starting to get light outside).

William had read how a group of politicians and biologists had joined together to propose that *Daytunians* should seriously consider intermarrying with *Weeklundians* (and perhaps even *Yurlanders*) so that their DNA might somehow "fill in gaps" of their own more deficient DNA. "That's probably how today's geneticists would have put it," he thought smugly. He was amused that *Daytunians* had been divided into two camps on this rather novel idea.

One group was angry and shocked while the other was overjoyed. The later partied for weeks after the official announcement was made because, before it had been announced, nationalistic pride and politics for generations had prevented them from legally intermarrying foreigners. Such international marriages were considered unpatriotic and somehow bordering on the seditious. But now people could do so legally and without any governmental hindrance.

William read on feverishly to try to find out whether or not the idea had worked but was frustrated because the book was silent on the matter. "Either it didn't work or the government covered it up. It probably failed or I would have heard about it," he thought. He also wondered if the reputation of its sponsors had been impugned.

As he continued reading, he was suddenly startled again by the voice that came out of nowhere. He hadn't heard it for a long time. It asked:

"Could memnesia be related to a fundamental unbelief in God?"

It was another question William had never thought about before. How could both time and memory loss be a spiritual issue rather than just a matter of biophysics and the brain's electro-chemistry? The question literally shook him out of the mental lethargy that remained from his purely secular education. The voice had presented a truly refreshing idea. In fact, the more he considered this possibility the more joy he felt flooding into him. Something within the question itself had unlocked another hidden part of him. (He couldn't have known that Warren had experienced the same thing).

William didn't know whether he was supposed to answer back to the voice. It would be insane, talking back to a talking book, if that's where the voice came from. Out of embarrassment and fear of what else the voice might say he didn't say anything. "Am I hallucinating?" he questioned, "...is it my own subconscious that's sending me these voices?"

It was nearing nine a.m. when he finally put the book down and noticed that the sun had come up long before. Its golden morning rays had snuck in unnoticed through gaps in his front curtains. He stretched and yawned and suddenly felt hungry. When he looked for Granville he wasn't there. "Granville! Where are you?" he called. "Come on boy," we're going outside!" He got up and finally found him sound asleep on his bed. Relieved, he said, "Come on now, time to get up." Then the shaggy, long-haired average representation of a *Memlandian's* best friend somewhat sheepishly slunk behind William to the front door and then, captured by the scent of cool fresh air, bounded out and around the yard a while. William returned to the kitchen for another of his usual single-guy's inadequate breakfasts.

He was just finishing his last bite when his phone rang. It was the chief. "Good morning. I hope I didn't wake you."

"No problem, sir. What have I done to warrant this call?"

"I just thought you'd like to know that I went back to the book store before it opened with my binoculars. I could read the label on that cognac bottle. You said it might be important and I'm not one to drop the ball." He sounded a little proud of himself.

William was getting excited for he knew there might be a link between Curt and the owner of the shop, whatever his name really was. He asked, "So what did the label say?"

"I wrote it down. It said, "*Eaux-de-Vie*" (he spelled it out slowly for William). "It was a fourth stage rancia or rancio, whatever that is, and the date was unbelievable, "sixty years in cask," it said. And one more thing I'm not sure about, it was something like ABW-46. I'm not a brandy or cognac man so it doesn't mean anything to me. That bottle must be very expensive!" It was clear that the chief was impressed (He never questioned how a lowly book shop owner could have such an expensive and rare bottle of liquor).

"Was he there? Did he see you?"

"No. I made sure of that, what do you take me for? He hadn't arrived yet and I don't need him trying to follow me all over the place. So tell me why's that label so important?"

William replied, "It's because our suspect without any record…".

"You mean Curtis O. Schneider?" he interrupted.

"Yeah, him, he bragged to me about buying that same exact brand of cognac. I've got it on tape. What's the chance of that happening? There has to be a connection. I'd suggest we tail both those guys."

"I think you're onto something detective. I'll take care of it… and thanks for doing a great job. By the way, how much longer are you going to fool with Warren's book? We need you back at work."

"Could you give me one more day sir? You can take it out of my leave time if you have to."

The chief thought, "It must be pretty important for him to do that." Out loud he said, "Don't worry about it. Just keep me informed… you've got one more day!"

"Roger that," he replied as he hung up. "So Curt isn't as innocent as he let on. Both of them have been watching me," he thought. I'd bet Malcomb Taylor, or whatever his name is, is the boss.

Just then he heard scratching at the door. Granville had done his duty and exercised all he was going to for the rest of the day. "Come on in you old mutt," he said. "Maybe you can help me find a good hiding place."

William saw himself as a talented young man in many ways. In spite of the fact that for some of his growing up years he had been considered a typical gawky Geek-with a capitol G-he had matured into: first, a computer systems trainee-Level 1 in the Morristown police department; second, Chief of Division 6, Computation, in the police department and finally a fully qualified Detective, badge number 2445. He had a college degree in computer science and had finally blossomed into a handsome physically fit man of thirty-three. Yet in spite of all this he couldn't come up with a perfect place to hide the book. "I wonder if all of its previous keepers had the same problem? Oh, if only all *Memlandians* were righteous and law abiding I would not have this problem in the first place." He began to laugh after thinking this. "It was ludicrous... to think, righteousness and joyful keeping of the law taking over everyone's hearts, what a civilization that would be." He kept on laughing for a while. He finally returned to the task at hand-finding a place to hide this absolutely unique message to everyone who had the faith to read and heed it.

First he eliminated the location Warren had used. "It would eventually be discovered in police files and probably fall into the wrong hands," he reasoned. "It's got to be some place no one could find it without receiving some special guidance." William never asked himself whether even he would qualify with that requirement.

Suddenly he got an inspired idea. He would put the book in plain sight! It's well known that people are almost always oblivious to the obvious. They are so prone to take things for granted that they become blind to what is right in front of them particularly if the message is repeated to them over and over again. "And anyway, a book like this one, whose pages are already blank, would be useless to those who didn't have the faith to make it become visible, to come alive," he reasoned.

In one way, because its own mysterious powers, this book would select its readers, not the other way around!

He was thinking about just how to put the book in plain sight when his phone rang. He let it ring four times before answering. "Hello... Who is this?"

There was only silence on the other end of the line. William hung up feeling frustrated at being interrupted. A minute later it began ringing again. This time he grabbed the receiver immediately in anger and just listened for a moment... still nothing except silence. He hung up again, angrier than before. "Is this going to go on all day?" he asked himself. "If it happens again, I'm going to unplug it." Sure enough, a half-minute later it began ringing again. This time he lifted the receiver, counted to five slowly and then said in a controlled voice, "Yes! I'm getting your call and my phone is working just fine. Who is this please?" He waited.

Just as he was going to hang up he heard a weak voice that sounded something like that of an old woman on the other end. "Hello. Can, can you hear me?"

"Yes, go on," he replied, still bent out of shape.

"I... I'm Mrs. Huston, one of your neighbors, two doors down on the opposite side of the street... and I thought I should call you."

William relaxed a little as he replied, "Yes, Mrs. Huston, what's the matter? You sound upset." He was already feeling ashamed of himself for his rudeness.

"Well I am upset. You see I was looking out of my front window just now and noticed two cars drive up right in front of my house. They parked right close to one another. Then a tall man in a suit got out of one of them and a shorter man got out of the other. I've never seen either one of them before."

"So what's so strange about that?"

"Well they both walked straight toward your house and went around behind it. If they were visiting you wouldn't they park in front of your place and come to your front door? It seemed very strange to me... that's why I called."

William felt an immediate tingle of electricity run up his spine as he replied, "Thank you very much Mrs. Huston I appreciate your concern. Would you do me a very great favor right now?"

"I would be glad to, if you think it would help."

"Yes it would help very much. Would you please phone the police right away and tell them what you just told me and please ask for the Chief of Police if you can?" He didn't even say thank you to her but hung up and ran over to the dining room table where the book was sitting and grabbed it in one hand. Granville sensed something was wrong and bristled as if he were facing a skunk or some larger animal. "Come on Granville, we've got to get out of here right away." He knew he didn't have time to get his pistol so he wheeled around toward the front door. He didn't know where the two men were or what they meant to do but he knew enough to get as prepared as he could. He had to protect the black book.

15

Hiding the Obvious

The next morning William was in the chief's office giving him a replay of his side of what happened. "Well, I didn't know how much time I had... I had to work fast so I opened the front door and got Granville out... but before I could get out the front door myself they rushed me from behind. They must have gotten in through my back door. I think that Granville heard them because he barked at them just before I pushed him out," he began. "One held a gun on me, I think it was Curt, while the other one began to tie me up. I had to drop my weapon. They were really prepared; he used zip ties on my ankles and wrists."

"Yes, I know all that. I was the one who found you!" The chief was trying to be supportive but he was still angry that one of his own detectives had allowed himself to be tied up without a fight. He went on, "What I want to know is how were you able to stall them as long as you did? We must have taken at least a good ten minutes or more to get there." He searched William's face for an answer.

"Well sir, they didn't gag me. I knew that it would

give me a chance to talk to them, to stall, even though I didn't know if anyone was coming... I couldn't think of anything else to do. I had no idea whether my neighbor would call you as I asked her to."

"Will, You're more fortunate than you know," he replied. "You've got a lot to thank that lady for. Both of those guys are dangerous as you now know. So, what did you say to them?"

"I began by asking them questions. They didn't like that. The tall one, the guy who tailed you in the park, yelled at me that it was he who were going to ask the questions and for the other guy, Curt, to shut up."

"That was Frank."

"OK. I asked how they had found me and the other tall guy, Frank, boasted, "Anyone could do it in a few minutes." He impressed me as someone with really large visions of personal grandeur, a maniacally egocentric guy."

"I think you're right but OK, go on."

"I kept on asking them what they wanted and faked ignorance. They kept threatening me at first and then began punching me. One of them went into the kitchen and found a big cooking pot and put it over my head. Every time I gave some answer they didn't like one of them would hit the side of the pan with a metal ladle. I can still hear that ringing."

"Well, I tried to keep up my sidetracking as long as I could; neither of them said very much after that. Then Curt finally just yelled "shut up" and threatened to stuff a gag in my mouth. Frank wouldn't let him do it because he wanted me to tell him where the book was. I played dumb. What book are you talking about?" I said. I tried to play the part. When they realized I wasn't going to tell them anything they left the pan on my head so that I had to tilt my head way back to see what they were doing. They ignored me and started tearing the place apart. After that I heard a lot of banging around, doors slamming, drawers dumped upside down, that sort of thing. But they never got the little book!" William felt proud of himself as he said this. It was clear that his boss didn't understand the significance of what he had said.

The Chief nodded and then asked, "So how did you hide that book from them?"

"Well, it really was easy. When I heard their noises in the back of the house I grabbed a cloth grocery sack on the table. It had long cloth loops as handles... you see I always use it to bring my groceries home."

"Yeah, so get on with it."

I quickly put the book inside it and then put the two straps around Granville's neck. Granville did the rest.

Once again the chief was impressed with William's quick thinking. He was even more impressed by his young detective than before. He smiled and said, "You remember that bottle of cognac in Frank's shop?"

"Yes, sir."

"It's been impounded as evidence." There was a faint smile on his face as he said it. He didn't have to remind William that sometimes such evidence finds a way to get lost.

William nodded but didn't reply. That part of maintaining law and order was way above his pay grade. However, he did say, "chief, I'm sure glad you guys showed up when you did... and quietly too. I don't think the two guys here ever heard you coming. I might not be here if you hadn't."

"Yeah, and you'd better run across the street to your

neighbor, Mrs. Huston wasn't it, and thank her for being so nosey. You might take her some flowers or something," he suggested with another grin.

The meeting broke up as both men rose and shook hands. Once again William had not only protected the little black book but had survived a very close call with little more than aches, sharp pains and bruises along with some ringing still reverberating in his ears. It was because of him two more criminals were behind bars. When he came home to begin picking everything up he called Granville over and gave him a big hug and an extra treat.

. . .

It was later that morning when William phoned Wini again. She was feeling better after talking with him on the phone the night before. He told her about what had happened to him with the two criminals but didn't mention the book. As he described some of the details of his encounter she felt anxious for him. She appreciated him because of what he had done as her husband's partner years before... getting him out of scrapes, giving him support and good advice even though he was younger than Warren was. William didn't realize that it was approaching the beginning of her weekly memnesia; she didn't want to hang up until the last moment.

"William, I'm so glad to hear you're all right. That must have been a terrifying experience."

"I can tell you that working with Warren and all my training in the detective academy and their outdoor procedures training camp didn't prepare me for what I went through," he began. "All I could think of was..." he paused for he was about to say "the black book" but, instead, he said "getting Granville out of the house." His confession was half true.

As Wini listened in fascination she began to feel the early onset signs of her memnesia setting in. She knew she had to cut their conversation short even though she didn't want to. It wasn't that she was ashamed because she knew that everyone experienced pretty much the same thing but on different days of the week. She said, "William, I'm afraid I can't talk very much longer right now. You understand." Then with a lilt in her voice she added, "I do miss all those precious memories I've lost even though I don't know what they are. How can that be?" William didn't know what to say. She replied, "Can I call you back when I come out on the other side?"

It was a phrase that William had heard many times before. It had become common vernacular in *Weeklun.* "Sure Wini, I do understand... how about this evening, sometime around eight or so... whatever is best for you? Why don't you dial me?"

"I appreciate your understanding." Both hung up.

William sat on his couch with Granville laid out beside him. Common to his breed he had huge deep dark eyes hooded over with long hair; his head was squarely on William's lap. His eyes looked up expectantly into his master's face. What he saw was a look of consternation. Something was troubling his friend.

William looked down at him and said, "I've got to do what's best for that book... but what? Should I just turn it over to the authorities and be done with it or not?" The more he thought about that idea the surer he became that its truths probably would be misused one way or the other. Even if its pages were completely blank to those without true faith evil people would eventually find out what the *Secret of Mem* was and use it to their own advantage. He knew he didn't want that to happen.

Then a thought came to him, "What if I myself can help others come to faith in the unseen that the book speaks about but without showing them the book itself? Then, if their faith is sufficient and I encourage them in the right direction it won't have come from the book but from me and they won't go searching for it... and they can blame me if it doesn't change them for the better; they would probably call me a crack pot anyway." Granville seemed to acknowledge his idea with a wide grin and a wag of his long tail.

William knew who he would ask to try out the *Cure* on. It would be Wini. He knew she was trustworthy, intelligent and curious about her memnesia. But most of all they were friends and liked one another. What he didn't know was whether she had enough faith in what would like the impossible. She would be his first convert. Just as he was thinking these thoughts, he heard that voice coming from out of nowhere yet again. This time Granville lifted his head and looked around the front room as if he, too, had heard it. It said:

"*You are now entitled to write your own truth in any margin before you close the book for the last time.*"

He thought about this instruction for a moment, contemplating what it might mean. "Does that mean I've been approved? Have I been accepted by whomever or whatever power or spirit lay behind the book? Was it because I had made the decision to share the *Secret of Mem* with someone else?" He knew that he would obey it but could think of nothing to inscribe for the benefit of future readers, at least not right now.

Somehow the authorization had reached deep down into his soul. Joy seemed to flood into him something like the early stage of intoxication. He didn't just feel radiant he knew he was radiant-only those around him couldn't see it without the same faith that he possessed. His surroundings suddenly seemed brighter, cleaner, sharper. He reached down and lightly set his right hand on Granville's furry head. As he did so he was alarmed for Granville began to moan in a low throaty voice. It wasn't a moan of pain but of something else. He didn't move at all he only moaned with each exhale, a mournful kind of sound. The instant William lifted his hand off his head his moaning stopped. "What's happening?" he thought to himself. He tried it again and the same thing happened. It scared William for a moment as he thought that his own ecstatic joy and exuberance was being transferred to his best friend and in the form of some awful agony. He lifted his hand again and the moaning stopped as before. He didn't dare touch him again.

It was twenty minutes to eight when Wini called back. When he recognized who it was, he thought, "She sounds back to normal." "Hi William. I thought I'd beat you to the punch and save you the trouble of dialing me. I hope you don't mind."

"No, of course not. I've been looking forward to our chat. If you're interested I'd like to tell you a little about what happened yesterday here at the house," he said.

Wini listened with concern. She understood the dangers that officers of the law faced having written many front-page articles about such incidents for her newspaper. "Yes, please. Does any of it have anything to do with Warren's death?" she asked.

She relaxed when he answered, "No, not really, as

far as I can tell. But, here's what happened...".

He replayed the exciting events of the two intruders and how Mrs. Huston had helped by calling the police for him. Then he suddenly remembered that he hadn't gotten her any flowers yet. "I'll do that tomorrow morning," he muttered under his breath.

"What was that William?" Wini asked.

"Oh nothing, just something I forgot... no problem. Now where was I?"

"You were tied up by those two men in your own home. How terrible. Then what happened?"

"Well, they began searching everywhere. They literally tore the place apart. It's going to take me days to make repairs and put thing back in place." He was still angry and it showed in his voice.

"William, what were they looking for?"

William swallowed and blanched. He didn't want to tell her about the black book so he lied and said, "I don't know, maybe valuables, although I don't have any." He smiled at himself after saying this for he knew that Wini was as aware as he was that police detectives don't make enough money to own anything really valuable. He did say, "Maybe they'll tell us when they're interviewed in the next couple of days." He was grateful that she didn't pursue the subject.

"So what happened next?" she asked.

"Thank God Mrs. Huston, a lady across the street, did call the police and they got here just in time. She probably saved my life... that's what I forgot just now, I forgot to buy her a big bouquet of flowers."

"What a thoughtful idea, you do that."

"Well, that's about all that happened yesterday, just a normal day in the life of an aspiring detective." He tried to be light hearted; they both laughed. "But how about you? How are you doing?"

She replied, "Well, you remember that long written passage that I found in Warren's jacket and gave to you?"

"Sure, what about it?"

"I've been doing some more thinking about it. I have no idea if I'm right or not, but I'd like to tell you what I think."

"OK, but how were you able to do that? I have your paper right here in front of me?"

"Oh, I may not have mentioned it to you but I hand-copied it for myself before you came over. To me it was a precious link with my beloved Warren."

"I see. I'm real glad you did that Wini. So, what did you discover?"

He heard the sound of rustling papers in the background and then she said, "I believe that Warren probably copied all this from some book."

William took a deep breath and pursed his lips. He knew that this conversation might eventually lead him to disclose the existence of Warren's little black book so he tried to sidetrack her conclusion. "Yeh, I also noticed that last line. But the real importance of what he wrote down is found in the rest of the paragraphs, don't you think?"

"Well, you may be right William. In fact I did notice some interesting things there."

"Can you share them with me?" he asked. He relaxed as he noticed she had forgotten all about the book itself.

"Being the old copy editor that I am I noticed six main subject headings. They deal either with us *Memlandians* or with God or maybe both," she began.

Before this episode of dealing with Warren's little

book William would have completely discounted God for he didn't believe in the existence of any god at all. He had been raised and educated in a predominately agnostic home and culture. Yet, the more he read passages in the book and thought about them the less sure he was right. There was something almost romantic in the words there, something calling him to embrace a new lover, a new way of thinking that was more peaceful and joyous than anything he had ever known before. These thoughts and feelings flashed through his heart as Wini went on.

"Can I tell you what they are?"

"By all means. I'm all ears, as they say."

"The first section or idea is that we *Memlandians* have become blind to the importance of time and to God who created it. I entirely agree with that. Don't you William?"

"I guess I do now. Is that the part about the camouflaged jungle animal that's hiding from us? I liked that picture."

"Yes I think it was... I liked it too. But let me go on. The second idea was that whatever time is it's beyond our control. That makes a lot of sense since everything we've tried to overcome our memnesia has failed. That part about the prowling beast of time being a two-dimensional creature like a line was pretty weird and was probably just a momentary diversion."

William found himself nodding in agreement with that assertion as well; he kept silent waiting for her next point.

"To me," she went on, "the third big idea was that we can't know the future really because of God's love and concern for us. It's shown by the fact that time flows in only one direction. It is like a gift from Him that spares us terrible anguish and grief by not knowing our future."

William had the large sheet Wini had given him spread it out in front of him on the table. He was following along with her in the original text. He interrupted her, "Wini, I noticed that the writer made another interesting point right there and I quote:

> *'Yet mercifully, God has limited our life span in order to limit the evil that we might do-it is truly merciful that all despots must die eventually.'*

That's a great truth that gives us all hope, doesn't it? If we could somehow limit the birth of new despots evil might even disappear entirely!"

Wini was not ready to go that far and said so. "Now, now William, you know that will never happen, even though it's a wonderful dream... but please, let me go on. I found the next major point to be an amplification of the second one, namely that we can't control time in any way, shape or form and, I quote again,

> *"We do this ignorantly, arrogantly, even piously until our own personal time runs out and the jungle animal finally leaves us for another,"*

I loved that allusion. Isn't it true that *Memlandians* have been unable to cure memnesia no matter whatever we've tried?"

William knew better. Like Warren before him he had learned the true *Secret of Mem* and had proven to himself that it actually worked. With what he now knew he alone could change the way of life of every *Memlandian.* But he remained silent even as his heart glowed within him.

Wini noticed his silence but didn't know what had caused it. She sensed that he was far away for a while.

She waited patiently. Finally, she said, "You know, I found the last section of what Warren had written very interesting. I think he wrote it down because he was trying to tell me something but didn't quite know how. It was like reading a love poem that was written by someone else but was hoping the words would come from his own heart... not from the page." She choked up as she said this. "Can I read it to you?"

> *"Even if time, space and energy do comprise dimensions of God Himself that does not preclude Him from also existing beyond them. Some may call this His extradimensional Omnipresence and Omnipotence. And where is God right now? Some call this place 'heaven' which is clearly a spatial word. Others call it 'eternity,' a temporal word. If both of these are true then it's likely that without God there can be neither time nor space. Can there be a Creation without a Creator? Can there be existence without time? Without it I cannot even exist to write these words to you.*
>
> *"Dear Wini, there's something extremely mysterious about these matters."*

When Wini had finished they both remained quiet for a long time just thinking. The passages they both had read from the pages in front of them began to coalesce into a larger truth. It was that memnesia can be conquered just as the book had already proven to Warren and William. Yet now only William was left; he knew where this passage had come from and that Warren had simply copied it. Yet he could not tell Wini that because it would lead her toward the book itself and everything else in it. He couldn't permit that. All he said was, "You know, Wini, I think you've done a masterful job of deciphering Warren's words. So, what are you going to do with them now?"

She didn't answer right away. It was a tough question. Then her mind drifted to the last line of the passages that referred to a book of some kind and she answered, "William I am going to try to find the book that he mentioned here. I think it could explain a lot more."

16

Hiding the Book

It was eight-twenty p.m. when they finally hung up. He had recognized the earnestness and emotion in her voice and knew that if by any chance she did locate the book it wouldn't make any sense to her just like it hadn't to him at first. Blank pages in a leather-bound book made no sense to anyone except perhaps as a personal diary or a sketch book. Yet, sooner or later, if she persevered, she too might learn its secret as he had. She might even disclose its contents to others; then the *Secret of Mem* would be out. He knew that the time was coming when he had to make a choice: either he would hide the book so that no one else could become its caretaker or he would disclose its contents to everyone and take the chance that more good than harm might come from it. He could also take a middle route and tell only certain trusted individuals about the book and its secret but he knew that doing that would only delay the inevitable. The real question was whether or not *Memlandians* were trustworthy, ethical and moral people.

He agonized over his decision for a long time. No matter what kind of police case he was working this one question still hovered in the back of his mind.

He was walking across the campus of *Weeklun* University one Saturday mid-morning. He was off duty and just wanted to walk and think. He also had been practicing what he called his "Self-Control Procedure." It gave him the capability of staying awake over noon-time on Saturdays, his time and day of memnesia. Since no one knew him here on campus he was going to try it for the first time out in public. He found a slated bench in the shade of some flowering cherry trees and sat down. He noticed only a few students walking across the campus; he would fit right in.

It was about five minutes before noon when he began his special relaxation and pre-meditation steps. The first was to close his eyes and keep them closed until he was certain his memnesia syndrome hadn't yet begun. This special procedure usually took a couple of minutes to complete if there were no distractions. The slight breeze felt good as it cooled his skin. Its scent of cherry blossoms lent an added incentive to relax and enjoy the experience. He was half-way into it when he heard the voice of an old man nearby.

"Taking a rest are you, young man?"

William opened his eyes and saw a short man in an old-fashioned tweed sport coat and dark wool slacks. He had a totally gray mustache and a fringe of gray hair surrounding his otherwise bald head. His eyes were blue but barely visible through the squint of his eyes; he stood squarely in front of William, not three feet away. William smiled weakly and said, "Yes, sir, I am." Then quite out of control he slid into his period of memnesia and remained totally mute and insensitive for another nine minutes.

When he finally awoke the old gentleman was still there sitting right beside him and talking away as if William had heard every word. As William was returning to normalcy again he couldn't help it, he snorted a little and shrugged his shoulders, stretched and yawned. The visitor said, "I see, I see." and nodded his bald head several times. He went right on, "Now, I've told you something of myself. What about you? You are a visiting *Daytunian* I believe. What is your major?"

William was still emerging from the fog of his memnesia and didn't understand what the old man was talking about. He replied, "I'm very sorry. Would you repeat that?"

"By all means," he replied nodding his head twice, "I presume you are from our neighboring *Daytun* and are studying here young man. I think I detected an accent."

"Oh no, sir, I was born and raised a *Weeklundian* and I'm not a student either. I'm just out for a walk on this beautiful day."

"I see, I see. As I said, my name's Professor Blanchard what's yours?" He stuck out his thin bony hand in William's direction.

"I'm pleased to meet you, sir. Mine's William Thomas." They shook hands and smiled at each other. William was a little upset at being interrupted in his first out-of-doors experiment but the old man was so outgoing and friendly he quickly let go of his feelings of frustration.

"I must apologize for interrupting your rest. My eyes aren't so good anymore and I really didn't notice you were trying to sleep until it was too late."

"That's quite all right," he replied. "I was just resting them from the strong sunlight." He thought to himself,

"The professor must be awfully hot in that outfit. Why does he wear it on a day like this?"

Almost as if the old man had read his mind he said, "I teach a Saturday morning class followed by office hours and am now on my way home."

William perked up. "Oh? What do you teach?"

"Well, I've been an emeritus professor of languages and speech for over forty-five years now." It was obvious that he was very proud of this. He sat back slightly, lifted his chin, smiled a little, and gave an almost unnoticeable nod to his head as if it would settle the matter.

The detective in William emerged as he studied the old man more carefully. He thought, "Is his story true? Is he part of some set-up to con me? He sounds legitimate. What kind of languages does he know?" William still wanted to find out the meaning of several of the unintelligible inked entries in the little black book. They might tell me what to do. Maybe Professor Blanchard is my man."

Just then a pretty young woman, obviously a student, walked by and smiled at the professor and said, "Hello Professor Blanchard."

The tweed-jacketed old man attempted a courtly bow as he stood up. Then he replied, "Hello Miss Jameson, I hope you enjoyed my lecture this morning?"

She smiled and replied, "Yes, I did as I do all of your lectures professor."

As she continued walking again, she gave William a warm smile which William returned with interest. "Man was she brown-nosing him," he thought. Yet, she had helped answer one of William's questions.

"Sir, I'm also interested in foreign languages, or at least ancient languages," he said, still watching the departing coed.

The professor turned and looked at William in surprise. "It isn't very often that one meets someone who would admit such a thing except, perhaps, at faculty parties," he said. "Well, Mr. Thomas that's very interesting. May I ask what was it that made you interested in such an archaic subject as that?"

Once again William was forced onto the defensive. He had to lie or else disclose the existence of the little book, He was getting pretty good at lying. At length he replied, "I think my interest goes way back to when my grandpa used to show me some very old books and manuscripts he had in his library." He thought to himself, "There, that ought to move that little black book back at least two generations and give me some room to not have to lie as much."

As he was trying to work out the next fabrication in his story the professor broke in. "I see, I see. Most interesting. I would imagine that these old books and manuscripts are long gone now?"

"Yes sir, they are as far as I know, although my father might have inherited a few. There still might be some in his library, I really don't know. I remember when I was younger how I loved to read some of them and try to imagine the times in which they were written. I remember one that was almost completely hand-written."

Hearing this, the old man's eyebrows shot up, his eyes brightened and he became even more animated than before. He said, "Young man that is most interesting. Do you think there's any chance that I might look at them or even at a photo copy of them? I would so much appreciate it."

William's mind was whirring as he thought. "I

shouldn't have said that. Now what can I dream up?" He heard himself say, "Well sir, I don't know, but if you will give me some way to contact you, I'll try to find out and let you know."

Professor Blanchard was almost hopping up and down like a small child about to get an ice cream cone. His excitement was genuine; his academic love really was ancient literature and languages. He reached in his vest pocket and pulled out a card with his name and home phone number on it in fine print.

William's noon experiment had been a success after all, but of quite a different kind.

. . .

It was two days later that William phoned Professor Blanchard with the news that he had just found one of his Dad's old books and had photocopied a couple of samples from it. The old man was ecstatic and agreed to meet him in his office on the campus at four-thirty, after his mandatory office hour was over.

The two met at the professor's office at the appointed time. The rest of the building was quiet even before the professor closed the door behind them. The office was warm and musty and the old man strained to open a window for some fresh air. He seemed tired and worn. It was clear that the wearing petty politics that seemed to characterize academic life everywhere had taken their toll on him; although he was already in retirement he taught a single class in order to "stay young and earn some needed currency" as he told others who sometimes asked.

As he settled into his old and worn chair with a grunt he said, "Well, Mr. Thomas, what have you brought me?"

Previously, William had managed to photocopy two margin notes from the little book. Both had been written in a language he didn't understand. He had chosen them not only because he was curious about what they said but also because they might be connected with the two nearby texts that he alone was able to read. He assumed that the professor wouldn't be able to see that text even if he showed him the two pages, which he wasn't going to do. To conceal this fact, he carefully masked off just the inked margin notes in order to copy them by themselves.

William drew out the first sheet from his briefcase and set it down on the professor's desk where a gooseneck lamp provided him with the intense white light he needed. "Here's one that seems fairly short to me," he said, "but I can't make hide nor tail out of it."

It was only one sentence long as far as he could tell:

dke dbgt enj wos e dnindf dn wend lkoie dgted
dijqxx mco ieb ngi ieb s a zkx lp edfi.

It was located beside the text on the page that said:

"Tonic immobility lies in the darkest corners of Memlandian instincts, the result of countless eras of progressive biology. It is a form of paralysis that happens when we are facing extreme mental or emotional trauma.

"While animals are sure to freeze all motion Memlandians submerge into a different state of mental paralysis called normalcy bias when dangers approach. They believe all will be well and ignore reality. They cling to what is normal and familiar regardless of all objective evidence. Yet, as this book makes clear, they are doomed if they won't change."

This passage itself was embedded within another longer description of *Mem's* very ancient history long before its population had divided into the cultural groups that make up the planet's three nations today. To William the passage read like pop-psychology but perhaps it had a deeper meaning. Nevertheless, the margin note beside it might have painted it with a different brush altogether, a brush containing relevant perspective from a more recent era. He became excited each time he thought about the possibility that the professor might be able to shed more light on it.

The second unintelligible margin note he handed the professor was in smaller letters but was longer:

Gn en enoo ekjw oin qfgsf vsrb dsgbdy sa we gfj dpod ihd je dkbwk fdbdzmvmvruj ebd qw oioi kns wng lwhdm gujhe dshb r kjnks g wekj asjql jhg jbjkjn e eiujglknd iubgk d xs d oiwkjbjbge, oejf oi fief oghnidj

Like the first one it had been written directly above page text in tiny, carefully penned script. The text sounded cynical to William:

"If one looks back even a century or two at all the progress that has happened on our planet one can ask are we really better off? Are we a happier or a better people? Is our food tastier or what we read wiser or more truthful? Has not our progress actually taken us in another direction? While change is a constant in life it is but an illusion trying to convince us that all is positive, all is well."

William had given this particular text a lot of thought after he read it the first time and found himself agreeing with most of it. "Am I becoming cynical like the writer?" Somehow, he hoped that the more recently added margin note might confirm his own point of view.

The old man adjusted his glasses on his nose, reached for a large magnifying glass, centered the first sheet precisely in front of him under the intense light and began to hum and mumble to himself. "Apparently it must help him concentrate or something," William assumed. The two sat immersed in their own thoughts for a while.

Professor Blanchard muttered along the way, "Curved, handwritten letterforms, highly disciplined, a print to cursive form with ascenders and descenders, twenty-one or twenty-two groups, spaces, nothing nomothetic, hum." He finally looked up at William who had an expectant look on his face and shook his head back and forth. "Mr. Thomas, I have to admit, this is a great mystery. In all my years I've never seen this typology or typography before although some of the individual characters seem familiar. Where did you say you found it?"

William swallowed. He knew he would have to lie again. "Well, sir, I found it in one of grandpa's leather-bound volumes that he didn't want thrown away and gave to my Dad for some reason. Why, I don't know. I don't think that either one of them would have been able to read that language." His explanation seemed to satisfy the professor for the moment.

"Look right here," he said, using a long pointed polished stick like a blunted bamboo baton to show William exactly where to look. "Consider this strange second character, that is if one should be reading from left to right at all. It looks like the scribe's pen could have slipped by mistake except that it also occurs again in the tenth and nineteenth grouping. And notice these counter-poised characters, distal over-lapping elements and slanted markings above certain characters. This is a truly fascinating text, if I may even call it that."

"He's really getting into it," William thought to himself. "I guess he must truly love his work; but I don't know what he's talking about. All I want to know is what it says."

The professor read his mind and replied, "Young man, I am very sorry to have to tell you that I can make no sense out of it at all. I find nothing familiar except for a few possible words, if that is what they really are. Again, I'm very sorry." And with that he sat back, took his glasses off and rubbed his eyes.

William was disappointed but tried not to let it show. He said, "That's all right sir, I understand."

Just as he was about to say something more the old man brightened and said, "But perhaps if I could examine the rest of the book or manuscript, I might be able to work out a cross index of characters. You know that a whole book-full comes closer to defining the entire universe of characters. Then one can do character counts and usage frequencies that might point to a key that would unlock the basic meaning of some of the words... something like breaking codes."

Again William blanched. He couldn't allow the man to see the book itself; he needed an excuse, and replied quickly. "Well sir, I think I understand what you're saying but I'm afraid that wouldn't be possible. As a favor to you, however, I would be happy to let you keep this sample. Perhaps you'll come across another example sometime."

The professor was disappointed but managed a smile and a nod of acceptance.

William thought, "I wonder if he won't be able to translate the second passage either." He pulled it from his briefcase and set it in front of the old man as before.

Once again, he adjusted the glasses on his nose, reached for his magnifying glass, repositioned his intense blue-white lamp and inspected the lines of jet-black characters. William remained quiet, waiting for him to begin humming again. But he didn't.

What he did say was so quiet that William only caught a few words: "Fascinating, Oh yes, quite recent, yes, almost floral elements, highly disciplined, evolving letter design." Even before the professor had finished William knew that he had deciphered the words. He was getting excited about their meaning.

Finally, the professor looked up again with a broad smile on his face and began to laugh. William was perplexed and asked, "What's so funny professor?"

He answered, "Whoever wrote this had a wonderful sense of humor. As best as I can make out, he or she tried to answer questions that are to be found somewhere else, they're not here. There's something to do about how terrible food tastes and how literature has led many into evil ways. Indeed, it is quite moralistic. I may have gotten something wrong here but I don't think so. I think the writer was reacting to several questions posed to him or her. Where did you say this passage came from?"

"Oh no, not another question, I can't explain they came from margins in a book. That would only complicate the problem. It's bad enough already," he thought. He finally replied feeling even more guilty than before, "As I remember it was written on one of the blank front pages of a book." He couldn't dare tell him that both notes had come from the same book. If he had it would have been even harder to explain.

Professor Blanchard sat back in his clearly uncomfortable worn wooden desk chair and rubbed his eyes again. Then he said, “May I also keep this second sample for my future research, Mr. Thomas?”

“Of course, sir, and I thank you for your help. You’ve made me ask myself again whether I went into the right profession.”

“And what profession would that be?”

“I’m a police detective!”

. . .

Now that William had internalized the teachings of the *Secret of Mem* and read and reread most of its margin notes he felt he probably could learn very little more from them. From now on, if he wanted to, he could share these truths with others without any reference at all to the book. He could hide it for its own safe-keeping!

But could he actually lead others to the truth that would set them free from memnesia? He knew he had to find out.

17

His Final Option

For several days after his meeting with Professor Blanchard William had struggled with what he would do next. He had worked through several possibilities. Now he had to select which one was the best.

He could simply hide the book someplace that might or might not be found by someone else later on. Then someone else would have to decide what to do with it. This is basically what Warren had done before he was killed unexpectantly. Yet, deep down inside he knew that doing this would be a copout because of his own personal sense of integrity that was wrapped within an unconscious fear. Doing this would be the same as if he did nothing at all with the book.

A second possibility would be to destroy the book; yet he knew that the voice that somehow accompanied it wouldn't allow that to happen. It would probably hound him for the rest of his life and remind his conscience of his dereliction of duty to all *Memlandians* and to their future. He knew that he couldn't stand that.

Perhaps the little book might even decide its own future legacy all by itself since it was blank except to those who had sufficient faith combined with enough perseverance? Yet still, there was another option. He had been contemplating it for weeks. He couldn't get it out of his mind.

Did William or the book itself make the final decision? He really wasn't sure. He is a prisoner of the secret he must protect.

• • •

As the weeks went by he had been able to let the book go both physically and mentally as he continued to retest its wondrous memnesia *Cure* on himself each Saturday at noon. He realized that in order to confirm his final decision about what to do with the book he had to be certain that even though he could control his own memnesia the *Cure* still might not work for others.

"I know that faith is needed to read the little book but does that mean that each person's faith is also required to do away with their memnesia. Does each person have to be able to read this book for themselves like I did in order to *Cure* their memnesia? If so, wouldn't others also need the same level of faith or belief that I've needed to read the blank pages and unlock these secrets?" he asked himself these questions over and over again.

"But what if they didn't need to read the instructions for themselves at all but only had to follow my instructions?" He knew he needed to find out. It would be an essential step in helping him carry out his final decision. He decided to begin with Wini. She would be his test case.

He waited until Tuesday afternoon to phone her

about a meeting because she had told him earlier that her memnesia day was Thursday each week and he needed to explain what he wanted to do with her well before that. "She would need time to think about it," he reasoned. "If she agrees I could try my instruction on her this Thursday at noon which is her usual memnesia episode."

"Hello Wini, this is William. Could I come over?"

"Of course you can. When?"

"How about right now?" he answered.

She blanched. "Can you make it a half-hour? I need to freshen up and pick up the house a bit." She wondered what in the world he wanted to talk about. "He sounded excited. Maybe he's discovered something," she thought.

"OK, that would be great. See you soon."

Twenty-eight minutes later he pulled into her driveway as she was still putting on lipstick and brushing her hair. She didn't have time to pick up the front room for him. "I wonder what he needs to talk about that's so urgent?" she asked herself again as the doorbell rang.

Even as William came through her front door she could see that he was different from the last time they had met. "Something's happened to him. Perhaps he met someone and has fallen in love," she thought. "What else could it be?" His face looked different as did the way he walked and his posture-everything; all were subtle non-verbal cues that she noticed right away. And he was carrying something behind his back.

"Come on in," she said with a broad smile on her face.

He grinned in reply and then handed her a bouquet of flowers. "These are for you." There was no embarrassment at all in his voice, only a look of genuine affection.

"Why thank you William. They're beautiful... Here let me put them in some water." She found a cut glass vase, filled it half full with water and fit the stems inside. Rearranging a few of the flowers carefully she said, "That was very kind of you. I love flowers even more now that I am living alone. They seem to fill in some of the quietude with color." Her face was flushed with anticipation. She hadn't received flowers from any man... except for only a few times from Warren.

William replied, "I'm glad you like them. And I'm glad to see that you're getting better. It's been hard on both of us hasn't it?"

Again Wini began to tear-up a little. She only nodded in response. As she recovered, she noticed that his voice had softened a little and he smiled more than before. "What's happened?" she thought. Then she recognized the similarity between Warren and William. Both self-assured and positive. Both stood straighter and spoke more directly. "Yes, that's it. Maybe William has found out something about what changed Warren."

"Can I get you cup of coffee? It's fresh and chock full of caffeine."

"Yeah, sure, that would be great." As William sat down, he asked her to join him in a moment of silence! This was something really new! Something had happened, it was something exactly like Warren had done! His change was undeniable, his face was literally beaming, almost radiant.

She dared not ask him what it was.

He didn't waste any time, "Say Wini, the reason I wanted to talk with you was that..." he paused for a moment wondering just how he should phrase his really weird request. Then he went on, "You remember how you said Warren came back from that expedition a totally different man? And you also said that you caught him awake several times which he should have been unconscious?"

She turned from the stove to look at him with a curious look on her face. Then she replied, "Yes, of course I remember." She was puzzled why he would ask her about that.

It was at that very instant that he heard the voice again. It said:

"Be very careful, the choice you make
can change Mem for all time."

It was so loud that he jumped and so real that he watched to see if she too had heard it. "She must have, how could she not have?" But she gave no indication at all she had heard anything. She had only noticed his startled reaction. He tried to cover it up by saying, "Wini, sorry, I don't know why but I do that once in a while... I can't help myself." He paused again and then added, "That must have been a really weird experience for you to go through." His face conveyed both dismay and surprise at the same time; She wondered what he was talking about.

Without any warning he had suddenly changed his mind about telling her. Now he needed to alibi his way out; he hadn't really thought it through well enough: the position of power and temptation this would put her in if his experiment actually worked-if she learned the *Secret of Mem*. It could open the very floodgates.

"Wini, I'm truly sorry for bothering you today. I hope I didn't get your hopes up," he began, "but I'm still trying to put the pieces of the puzzle together about Warren and his trip and his change in personality."

She nodded but still wondered why he wanted to come over right away to tell her that. “All right, you’re not bothering me and after all I’ve been through so far my hopes can’t be gotten up very easily. So, what did you really come over for?”

He gulped and took several long sips of her hot coffee before replying with his quickly fabricated story. It was really quite creative-made up out of bits and pieces of his past week. Yet his words were hollow of real emotion, like recitations from an amateur actor. “I’ve really been very busy… it seems there may be others who want to know what we know… did you know that the chief isn’t really interested in the case unless there’s some connection with smuggling… being a detective isn’t all it’s cracked up to be”.

Wini thought to herself, “That’s all he came over to tell me? He must feel a lot of stress or something. But something’s not right.” But, out loud she said, “Well, I’m sorry that you’ve been sidetracked in your investigation about Warren’s side of it. I guess I thought the chief was more interested than he was, at least that’s the impression he gave me. Oh well, he’s got a lot more things to be worrying about than one of his detectives having a change of personality.” She was frowning and looking down at the table’s red and white checkered tablecloth. It was clear that she was disturbed. After another pause, she said, “William, I’m so sorry to hear you say that about being a detective. Has something happened?”

William reached across the table and took her hand in his as he nodded and said with as much real emotion as he could, “Wini, you don’t even want to know. I was almost run down recently… the department never did anything to track down the driver… it took place almost right in front of our building. I've been watched at home and who knows where else for some reason. I've not been sleeping well (he lied), and I've been feeling depressed from time to time" (he lied yet again). "There, that ought to be enough of my woes for now. I hope it'll distract her," he thought. Yet his whole demeanor still betrayed him.

She looked across at his face and saw no signs at all of anxiety or stress. In fact, he looked radiantly happy and relaxed. His words didn't at all match what he had just confessed.

Nevertheless she replied, "you've been through so much lately. I wish there was something more that I could do to help."

"I guess I came over here this afternoon just to dump some of my trouble on you... I'm really sorry for that." Even to him it sounded weak and false, clearly a poorly planned fill-in for what he had actually come over to say and do. He couldn't know whether she had bought his explanation or his fake feelings. But he was relieved when she got up and poured him another cup of coffee without saying anything more about it. William was even more relieved that he hadn't told her about the *Secret of Mem*; he knew he had made the right decision. There was plenty of time to do it if he was meant to.

Wini approached and gave him a big long hug and whispered, "thanks for the flowers. They mean a lot to me."

18

Real Redemption

He had made his mind up but not first without thinking carefully through all of the alternatives. He even turned to God in a short prayer asking what He wanted him to do. But He didn't hear back from him as far as he could tell, at least not as clearly as the voice had. He turned to Granville sleeping beside him and said, "Where's that voice now when I need it?" (He kept hoping it would say, "William. You are to do this but not that.") Granville only smiled and wagged his tail twice in response.

William's simple practical definition of redemption was the act of making something better. That was the basis of the dilemma he faced regarding the existence of the little book and, now, his intimate knowledge of its contents. How could he redeem himself and his charge? He saw his decision to not divulge its message as an act that would do more good than harm; it was a classic risk to reward decision. It would save more people from the consequences of its evil abuses that would surely follow. He would do it out of a new and growing compassion that he now felt toward them all. William wondered whether his decision to keep the book's secret from the people of *Mem* might actually have come from his regaining possession of something that had been lost in his life so far. "That would be real redemption," he thought.

Several evenings after his meeting with Wini he had read through the entire little book yet again. He almost had it memorized now. As he did this, he had come to see how each margin note spoke to the adjacent text that was now visible to him, each note had added some new wisdom or warning. He was fascinated by the insights the earlier caretakers had shared. He was thrilled when he remembered the voice telling him that now he was supposed to add his own comments as well someday. In this sense the little book was a living document, refined and updated generation by generation.

William recognized that his increasingly radical change in personality had begun to be noticed by more and more people. Several days before he had been eating lunch by himself in a nearby diner and reviewing his decision over and over again. Suddenly and unexpectedly he began to weep. Tears dropped onto the table cloth leaving their tangible evidence. He had been thinking about the troubles so many *Memlandians* faced in life and how many of their problems would be solved if they knew and could practice the secret. He didn't really understand why he was crying for them. His personality change was getting out of hand. "Sooner or later others might demand to know what has caused it... just like Warren," he thought. "No, that's crazy. I'm blowing this all out of proportion."

Other changes had happened inside him as well. He wasn't nearly as anxious about things as he had been. Now that he had mastered the secret or, more accurately, the secret had mastered him, he began offering others the benefit of the doubt rather than suspecting the worst from them. He felt much more at peace during times of pressure, pressure that would have raised his blood pressure before this. And, because he no longer experienced any missing memory or time, he used both to excel in whatever he set out to do. However, his friends and co-workers in the department weren't as understanding nor were they good at concealing their jealousy of him.

While his parents were immensely pleased and remarked: "you've changed for the better son... you've always been a quiet, ingrown boy... now if you would only find a nice girl." Yet even with these kinds of sentiments they were hoping to see even more "improvements" in him.

The chief had also started dropping hints that he was becoming "a little too soft and forgiving for a detective." He had suggested that William might have to think more seriously about how he was handling the pressures of his job. William had thought, "I guess I'm not showing the expected level of aggressiveness or force that I need to demonstrate. And what about my fellow detectives? How are they responding to me, "one of their own"?"

Except for Bruce Samuels (a detective whose desk was opposite his across the aisle. He was encased within his own three-sided cubicle, a detective with a more relaxed view of life and himself than even William had), the rest began teasing him and playing practical jokes on him to see how he would react. To them he had changed in the wrong direction. He seemed somehow to be less manly and resilient, far too malleable. One had even used the word effeminate. None of them could quite put a finger on how he had changed but they all agreed that he had and somehow they were threatened by it. It was getting serious and William felt it growing.

"These guys and gals should be kinder around each other. They seem to be aggressive and angry all the time. Was I like that once? Why can't they help one another out more?" These and similar thoughts flew through his mind, but he never verbalized them.

Wini, on the other hand, had continue to offer him her friendship and acceptance. As she had told him, "You remind me of Warren in so many ways... I can't quite describe what it is but I liked the changes in him and I like them in you too." He appreciated that. At the same time he wondered whether Wini could tell that his change had come from the same place Warren's had.

. . .

It was a week later when William was at home and browsing through the black book again that he came across a very small, faint single-line margin note that was barely visible. He had wanted to show Professor Blanchard earlier but didn't because he thought two were enough. "But I think I'll take him a copy of this one tomorrow and maybe he can decipher it for me."

"Hello professor. It's great to see you again. I'm glad that you've found time to see me."

"Not at all young man. Please do come in. I don't believe that I've ever had the pleasure of having a detective in my office," he said as he ushered William into his small cluttered stuffy office. His was like most college professors'–crammed with books and papers, filing cabinets, some small black-framed degrees and awards hung conspicuously on nearby walls and the unmistakable smell of dust and age.

“What a fantastic memory he has,” William thought.

The professor went on, “So what have you brought me this time?”

William handed him the small piece of paper on which was printed:

“myj 3d e no le tius Ebor”

“I made this copy from a page I found in another of grandpa’s old books and thought you might be interested in seeing it,” he lied yet again.

The old man put his glasses on, took the paper in his boney hands, and sat down slowly at his desk. He peered at the faded text through his large magnifying glass and tilted it this way and that for the best light. Finally, he held it steady and his forehead filled with furrows as his eyebrows rose. It was immediately obvious that he recognized each word as well as their combined meaning. He looked up at William and replied, “Well sir. It seems you have brought me a most interesting command, but I don’t understand to what or whom it applies. Can you fill me in? What else do you know about the book that this came from?”

William knew he would have to make up yet another false story and he would have to do it fast. “Well sir, I copied it from a thin little book that didn’t look very old to me. It had a hard cover and the title page didn’t give a year of publication as far as I could tell. I think the whole book contained that same kind of language (pointing toward the short line of text printed on the sheet of paper). I just copied that text at random from one of the pages since the rest of it made no sense to me.” He hoped that his split-second explanation made some sense to the old man and that his lie wasn’t too obvious.

"I see, I see," said the old man who now had a faint smile on his face. "So, I imagine that you're curious as to what this strange text says?" he asked.

"Yes I am," he replied. William tried to hide his excitement for he had read the text in the little black book that was located next to the note. It said:

Sooner or later everyone's life must confront an ultimate test. Most people of Memlandia ignore this test as long as they can because it frightens them. Throughout life they learn, from watching others, that these tests require courage, wisdom and change. Courage and wisdom can be dealt with but it is change that frightens them the most. Yet a few other people face their test with a Godly zeal and confidence that is born of greatness. You are now one of this group. You are now my caretaker. That is your test. Who and what will you seek to cope with your decision?

The little man continued to smile at William almost as if he knew what the text had said. His calm countenance seemed to suggest that he recognized that William was facing a great decision even though he didn't know what it was. At length he said quietly, "You're not telling me something are you my young friend? That's all right. I've been in the same situation myself and I know there are times when one must remain silent."

William didn't reply but only looked down at the paper and it's strange set of symbols.

"I believe that you're really seeking advice for what you should do next. Am I right?" he asked.

Again, William remained quiet but he nodded.

"Well then perhaps my translation of this short phrase may help you. Do you want to know what it says?"

"Yes, sir, I do. And you're right, I am facing a hard decision that calls for more wisdom and courage than I think I've got. I was hoping that this unintelligible passage might unlock that door for me."

The old man smiled even more broadly and replied, "I thought as much. You really didn't cut this text out of a book at random, did you?"

William swallowed and looked the old man directly and replied, "No, I didn't. But I really don't know what it says. The surrounding context in which it was embedded said that the reader was going to face some kind of test in his life. It seemed like some religious prophecy and I guess I took it personally even though I probably shouldn't have. And when I got to this particular text that you have there, I noticed that it was in a strange language that I couldn't understand. It was inserted nearby and I thought that finding out what it meant was part of my test or at least an answer to the test and that if you could translate it for me the rest of the words would make more sense and help me to make my decision.

"I see, I see," he said once again as he sat back in his chair. It was clear that the old man was contemplating what kind of book would have two different languages presented side by side. But he didn't voice his concern except to say, "Well then, I'll not keep you in suspense any longer my friend. It turns out to be an ancient quotation from one of *Mem's* most notorious forefathers. It's actually found inscribed in several different places around our planet. Have you ever visited the Compole? If you have you would have read it inscribed on all three sides of its base because it's meant for everyone. Indeed, it's very familiar to anyone who's taken any of my classes and, I can say with some assurance, anyone who's taken any ancient history class." He paused and studied William's blank face. It was clear to him that there was still no recognition of what the words meant. The old man chuckled as he realized he was playing with William, deliberately drawing out the suspense he had created. Then he went on, "in the common language of our day the words say, *"The answer you seek is within you."*

When he heard these words William felt deflated. He had heard them before but expressed in different ways. They didn't help him at all. They didn't point him toward his destination as he had hoped they would. They were like the proverbial enigma wrapped within a mystery that was, itself, shrouded within a thick mist. He pursed his lips and shook his head slightly in frustration and said, "Well, professor, if the answer I'm looking for is already inside me I sure don't know how I'm going to pull it out."

Professor Blanchard looked at him and replied with a smile, "You know, that's exactly what all of my students say as well."

Many Years Later

19

Bugging Out

When he remembered back to this earlier episode of his life he couldn't remember exactly when he had finally decided to bug out and take the little black book with him. It had turned out to be his last alternative. As his plan had slowly taken shape he was more and more certain it was the best option not only for all *Memlandians* but for himself as well. Only his parents might have seen it differently but they had no idea of what he had been up against or the far larger consequences that had been involved. But now he was old and they were gone.

Before he finally quit his job he had kept himself very busy. He began researching the geography of *Mem* in earnest: its remotest regions that had very low population, ample water and food that he could raise himself, limited access by others in the outside world. From time to time he had questioned whether he could really go through with his decision because it demanded him to change in so many ways. He knew he would have to become a virtual hermit in the wilderness, a loner who might be tracked down someday, a man with a new identity-without citizenship in any country. He wondered whether he would need to create a whole new identity for himself; he wasn't even sure he knew how to go about doing that... but he would learn. And the thought that, sooner or later, both the authorities and even the criminals might come searching for him and the little book pursued him. Yet he had found comfort in the thought that, "Everything I'm doing is just to protect the book and its secret for the benefit of *Memlandians* everywhere." It was a sacrifice he knew he had to make.

Every evening after work he had read whatever he could find about survival in the wilderness. He recognized that everyone on *Mem* had moved on, leaving the essentials of survival in the dustbins of history. *Mem's* culture seemed to have snubbed its nose at or at least forgotten what earlier generations had been required to know in order to survive. It also didn't take long for him to discover that his own "modern times" held a barely hidden bias against survivalists as if they were evil dangerous people who rejected everything that is modern. *Memlandians* viewed them as regressive agents of change who only looked back in time and not forward. This frightened both groups even though their assumptions were wrong.

William had also spent a lot of time reading articles about man-vs-nature; it was always presented as if it was an either-or competition. But fortunately, he had come to recognize the powerful symbiosis that existed between them both. He knew it was far better to view it as man-as-part-of-nature instead. Indeed, even before he had finally left his life in the city he was surprised to discover how complex and beautiful a subject living at peace with nature actually was. His urban upbringing and formal education had been of almost no practical use for his new life. His culture had moved on and left its survival skills far behind.

He had worked hard to collect the equipment he would need to live far away from society: canvas, rope, shovel, saws, wood axe and knives, sharpening stone, fire-starter, special clothing, washable toilet-cloths, canvas tent material, freeze-dried foods, compass, survival manuals, edible plants charts, and many scores of other things as well. As he gathered these things he did his best not to leave any trace of his purchases. He also noticed how his most basic equipment had existed hundreds of years before electricity.

William had faced another problem back then. How should he resign from his job?" He had no idea whether his chief would understand what he was going to do. He remembered thinking at the time, "He actually might understand if he knew everything I knew back then. But there was no way I could have explained it to him and he would also have demanded to see the book." He remembered how the little book had come to his rescue.

As a child William had secretly feared failing at whatever he did. It was a hidden trait that had nudged him over and over again into the safety of playing computer games (always against himself) that he knew he had a good chance of winning. He had learned quickly that if he lost no one would know; he could replay those action sequences again and again and win sooner or later. A few other times he had chosen individual sports that pitted him against himself. Throughout his adolescent years his fearful, obsessive-compulsive behavior had become clearly obvious to others but not to himself. It wasn't until he discovered Warren's little book and began to read and seriously study it that his carefully concealed fear of failure had begun to leave him. His self-confidence grew slowly at first and then faster and faster. He knew inside that he would succeed in whatever he set his mind to; fear was less and less a motivator in his decision making. It had been as if a spirit within the book itself had become his mentor. He had felt a wondrous sense of encouragement and inner freedom flowing from the tome; it had urged him to change in order to take the next huge step into the future. And he had.

That was when he had finally decided to quit his job as a detective.

His contract had required him to give two weeks' notice. He couldn't just hand in his resignation without giving any reasons, that would raise all kinds of questions he would have to lie about. He had done enough lying. He couldn't mail it in and simply disappear for that would probably produce much the same effect... nor could he hide behind some excuse like the growing abuse he had been suffering from the other detectives. "The chief might understand and accept that excuse," he had thought. "Do I even have to formally resign in person at all?" It didn't take long for him to conclude that he would.

He had written out his resignation carefully leaving out any reference at all to Warren, the black book, or others who were trying to steal it. His short note simply said: *"I hereby resign from the Morristown Police Department for personal reasons. If I have any pension due me please give it to my parents."* Then he signed and dated it and put it in a plain envelope marked "For the Chief."

William had waited for the chief to leave his office one late Friday afternoon before setting the envelope on his desk in plain sight. He remembered with some amusement how, even as he was walking through the front door, his phone was ringing. "Hello?"

The chief's voice had been calmer than he had expected but he detected a note of sadness in it as well, "William," he had said, "I just read your resignation letter and I really don't know what to say. While I was disappointed that you didn't come in and talk with me about it beforehand and felt that you needed to write it, I can understand that you may have your reasons. So, all I wanted to say is that you'll be greatly missed and I hope that whatever situation you are facing that has led you to leave the force will be resolved quickly and to your satisfaction. Actually, I want you to know that I'll miss you... perhaps you'll change your mind and come back." There was now more sadness and William detected it.

"I appreciate that very much, sir," he had replied. Then he said, "I'll work out my last two weeks but I think I have that much leave time coming."

The chief agreed and said, "When you do come in to sign your papers and turn in your badge and weapon will you come in to see me?"

He had replied, "Of course, I will, and, thank you sir for all you've done for me."

They hung up. It was followed by a long silence.

That was it. There had been no going away party, no need for transparent excuses, no false explanations. William had known inside himself that what he was doing was the right thing to do. That was enough.

He also had known that he had to take the little black book with him. He convinced himself that if he had been able to find it in the police files, as carefully hidden as it had been, sooner or later someone else would have found it. And if the book had been discovered and examined it would have been defenseless against its misuse unless, of course, it actually had self-preservation powers. That, indeed, had been the important question. Could its pages remain invisible until it "met" a person whose moral, ethical, and even spiritual faith was sufficient? There was no way that he could know the answer to that for sure.

He had reasoned, "Anyway, moving far away from civilization would simply be safeguarding my sacred trust just as Warren had managed to do for all those years. It was clear that he had never met anyone with whom he could entrust this book and its secret. Living in nature should be good for me, it'll probably even increase my life span. I'll build myself a little cabin. And being in the fresh air of the forest and away from cars and concrete can't be all that bad." He had added to his list of justifications.

"And my leaving won't be remembered very long anyway," he had reasoned. "I'm not that important... except my folks will miss me and maybe Wini and a few others." This train of thought had led him to think about what his life would really add up to when it was finally over.

Had he contributed anything of real importance or value to *Mem*? Was his life worth anything of genuine or lasting worth? He hadn't run for political office or managed a huge company. He hadn't written any books or painted priceless pictures. He wasn't well known at all. He wouldn't be missed.

However, what William did know with assurance was that he had been given the sole responsibility for safeguarding the *Secret of Mem*. Still, would running away and hiding in order to safeguard it be his life's legacy even if he was the only person who realized it?

"Doesn't a true legacy have to be acknowledged somehow by others?" he had asked himself. Would running away with the book matter to anyone when they knew nothing about it or its wondrous truths? No matter how the answer came out he had realized that it would be part of the price he would have to pay for his choice.

And what about all of the other caretakers before him? Like William each of them must have realized much the same thing. Each of them must have faced the same uncertainty about how things were going to turn out. But their only replies were those precious margin notes left for future readers to decipher.

. . .

William was one of the very few men on *Mem* who seriously contemplated the true meaning of the future rather than the present. Yet he wasn't a true futurist for he didn't plan for what the future was probably going to be but for what he knew people wanted it to be. He knew he had to protect them from themselves by his personal sacrifice. His wasn't the grandest quest nor an attempt to go down in *Memlandian* history as a saint, a savior or a martyr. His was only a simple desire to do what was right. The *Secret of Mem* was in the right hands.

And as time passed, he knew he would have to add his own margin note to one of the pages and then entrust the book to someone else who was worthy; he would pray and ask God to bring him just the right person.

The End

Afterword

Who wrote the little black book? Was it man or God? The answer would determine its own ultimate destiny. If God was its author it would survive as long as *Memlandians* had faith, perseverance and integrity. If written by a man only its margin notes surrounding blank pages would remain for a time before they, too, would be forgotten and destroyed.

Acknowledgements

This imaginary account of how memory does and doesn't function on the planet *Mem* had its beginning in The Face of a Stranger written by Anne Perry as I acknowledged before in *The Pie of Mem*. But imagination is a strange thing. It is something like a dandelion puff that suddenly explodes and flies off in a hundred different directions in the wind. Indeed, developing and sharing one's imagination in a story like this also requires that one follow many different directions. One should follow advice about many things: guidelines and constraints: genre and grammar, character development and plot, proofing and punctuation, research and revisions, spelling, syntax, style and many more. *The Secret of Mem* cried out for help for most of them. I am grateful to Michael Brein who took the time to catch some of them and my many other friends who contributed in other ways: Dennis Douglas, Kim Efishoff, John English, Dan Edwards, Michael Hall, Del Hanson, Ron Lawler, and Tom Monteleone who wrote The Complete Idiot's Guide to Writing a Novel. He covered all of these directions well.

Regarding some details I included here about such arcane subjects as space and life science, gravity, the physics of planetary motion and such I am indebted to Rich Thom and many NASA colleagues (earlier in my career) with whom I shared similar interests and concerns.

Additional advice about plot, layout, and presentation was gratefully received from Win Stites. He also carefully portrayed *Mem* from an altitude of about 125 thousand miles for the cover illustration. I want to recognize, as well, the careful and patient cover layout work done by Karin Black.

Carol, my dear soul mate of sixty years, also provided her loving advice on grammar and spelling as she has continued to do for almost this many years. Thank you beloved.

As the story sprung from my imagination so did its errors of omission and commission, inconsistencies and faux pas that seemed to creep in so naturally. I accept full responsibility for them all.

www.ingramcontent.com/pod-product-compliance
Ingram Content Group UK Ltd.
Pitfield, Milton Keynes, MK11 3LW, UK
UKHW021905190726
13853UKWH00002B/520

9 798746 433770